FOUL PLAY

Suddenly Martina's left foot came out from under her and she fell. Martina sat on the ice for a minute, stunned. How could she have messed up such an easy jump? Then she spied her left skate. Sure enough, the lace had come undone.

"Cut!" the director cried. "Take it from the top again, Martina! We're way behind schedule today, so hurry!"

Martina bent down to pull her laces tighter. A sense of dread went through her as one of the laces snapped off right in her hand. Martina saw the impatient look on the director's face as Blake went to get Kirsten, the costume designer, to inspect Martina's skates.

"Did you cut the laces?" Kirsten asked as she relaced the skates with a fresh pair.

Martina's eyes widened. "No! Why?"

"These were definitely cut," Kirsten said, showing Martina part of the broken lace. "Someone cut them partway. When you skated, they broke completely."

ICE
MAGIC

Melissa Lowell

Created by Parachute Press

A SKYLARK BOOK
NEW YORK · TORONTO · LONDON · SYDNEY · AUCKLAND

With special thanks to Darlene Parent, director of
Sky Rink Skating School, New York City

Cover costume by Tania Bass, New York City

RL 5.2, 009–012

ICE MAGIC

A Skylark Book / May 1996

Skylark Books is a registered trademark of Bantam Books,
a division of Bantam Doubleday Dell Publishing Group, Inc.
Registered in U.S. Patent and Trademark Office and elsewhere.

Silver Blades™ is a trademark of Parachute Press, Inc.

ISBN 0-553-48361-7

Published simultaneously in the United States and Canada

Bantam Books are published by Bantam Books, a division of
Bantam Doubleday Dell Publishing Group, Inc. Its trademark,
consisting of the words "Bantam Books" and the portrayal of a
rooster, is Registered in U.S. Patent and Trademark Office and in
other countries. Marca Registrada. Bantam Books, 1540 Broadway,
New York, New York 10036.

1

Martina Nemo dropped her dark brown eyes down to the ice of the Seneca Hills Ice Arena. She performed a near-perfect layback spin with her back arched to just the right angle. Martina loved practicing the difficult skating move—especially when she got it right.

Small wisps of her jet-black hair brushed her cheek as she came out of her spin. Martina was surprised to hear cheers and whistles from the bleachers. She glanced up and giggled when she saw her friends. The skaters in Silver Blades were used to rising early to get in morning practice before school. Silver Blades was one of the top skating clubs in the country. Its members were serious skaters.

Still, Martina had started practice a little late that morning. Her friends were already finished. They had changed back into regular clothes and were ready for school.

"Yahoo!" Nikki Simon cheered as she waved her arms over her head. "Way to go, Tee!"

"Bravo! Bravo!" Haley Arthur chimed in. Beside her, Amber Armstrong and Tori Carsen were clapping and whistling.

Martina stuck her tongue out at them. "Give me a break, you guys!" she called cheerfully. *The way they're carrying on, you'd think I'd just skated an Olympic program,* she thought with a smile. *But it was only her usual morning practice routine.*

Kathy Bart, one of the coaches for the club, checked her watch. She smiled at Martina. "Nice finish, Martina. That's all for now. Have a good day at school."

Martina skated off the rink and dropped down on a bench to catch her breath. That morning's practice had been especially tiring. *Maybe I shouldn't have stayed up so late last night,* she thought. *But it had been so much fun rehearsing with her father that she hadn't noticed the time.*

Mr. Nemo was playing the role of Danny Zuko in the Seneca Hills Community Theatre production of *Grease*. Acting was his hobby. Every evening after dinner, Martina and the rest of her family helped him rehearse his lines.

Most of the time their rehearsals ended up as huge laugh-fests. Martina's sixteen-year-old brother, Richard, was a total clown. The previous night he'd had them all rolling on the floor with his imitation of a strict school principal. Thanks to Richard, the rehearsal had ended later than usual. Now Martina was paying the price.

Martina stretched her aching back. Her friends climbed down the stands.

"I'll be ready in a sec," Martina told them.

Nikki Simon tucked her wavy brown hair under her hunter-green baseball cap. She swung her skate bag over her shoulder. "You looked awesome today, Tee," she said. "Your spins are so *tight!*"

Martina smiled. Nikki was her best friend from Silver Blades. They had gotten especially close lately. Nikki had even made up a new nickname for her—she was the only one who called her Tee.

Martina and Nikki enjoyed a lot of the same things: swimming, sappy movies, and horror novels. And though Martina hung around a lot with Haley, Amber, and Tori, she was definitely closest to Nikki.

"Your layback position was great," Amber said. Amber was only eleven, but she sometimes saw things that only the coaches noticed. She pushed her brown hair behind her ears with a sigh. "I have so much trouble with that spin."

Martina shrugged uncomfortably and mumbled, "Thanks." She'd never been able to take a compliment well. They always embarrassed her.

"Really, Martina," Haley said, "your forward layback is great." Tori nodded in agreement. Unlike Martina, Tori usually had trouble *giving* compliments.

Martina stood and ran her fingers through her chin-length hair. "So, hear anything today?" she asked.

The girls knew what Martina was talking about. For

weeks that had been the question everyone in Silver Blades was asking: "Hear anything about the movie?"

They meant a made-for-television movie called *Ice Magic: The Luci Ramirez Story*. It was going to be filmed in the Seneca Hills Ice Arena. *Ice Magic* was about the life of Luci Ramirez, a famous skater who was a star with the Ice Capades.

"I still can't believe that Luci Ramirez actually grew up right here in Seneca Hills," Tori said.

"Me either," Haley agreed. "Maybe we could become as famous as she did."

"Sure." Martina grinned. "All you have to do is win a gold medal." Everyone laughed. Luci had won her gold at the Winter Olympics in the 1970s. She had been fourteen years old—the same age as Martina, Tori, and Nikki.

"Well, I think it's cool that she was a member of the very first Silver Blades skating club," Haley told them.

"It's very cool," Martina agreed. "But it would be even cooler if any of us got into this movie! Waiting to hear is just about killing me."

"You? What about *me*?" Tori asked. "It's been six weeks since I sent my videotaped audition to the director in Hollywood."

Martina and Nikki exchanged amused glances. Tori always acted as if everything were about her. All of them had sent tapes at the same time. They each hoped to be cast as one of the movie's two skating doubles. Blake Michaels, the choreographer for Silver Blades, had been hired to create the skating scenes for the film. Blake had retired from amateur skating at age twenty-three to become a choreographer. He was in charge of sending the audition tapes to the production company. Now Blake and the skaters were waiting to hear who would be chosen as the movie's skating doubles.

"I've got to change. Wait for me," Martina called to her friends. She headed for the locker room.

In the locker room, Martina pulled her favorite over-sized navy sweatshirt over her button-front jeans and threw her workout clothes into her skate bag. She slammed her locker shut and sighed. She'd give *any-thing* to win a skating part in the movie. Luci Ramirez was her idol. She was the reason Martina had gotten into skating in the first place.

Martina picked up her skate bag and left the locker room to meet her friends.

"We were just wondering," Tori told her when she came out. "Don't you think the director will pick the absolute best skaters? Probably only those of us who can do a double axel."

Martina shrugged. It was obvious that Tori thought *she* was one of the best skaters in Silver Blades, and so the director would most likely pick *her*.

"I don't know," Martina replied.

"Well, I'm pretty sure I've got a good chance at being cast," Tori told them. "My audition tape was amazing. And I wore my purple outfit for it."

Martina grinned. Tori was an excellent skater. And she *did* have the nicest skating costumes—thanks to her fashion-designer mother, who made them all. But Martina didn't think the director of the movie cared about what Tori had worn during her audition.

Besides, Martina didn't really think Tori had much of a chance of being cast. Tori didn't look anything like Luci Ramirez. In fact, Martina believed *she* had a better chance than Tori because of her Hispanic heritage. Like Luci Ramirez, Martina's family was from Puerto Rico. And, like Luci, Martina had a light olive complexion.

Martina didn't point this out to Tori. Tori had obviously made up her mind that *she* would get the part.

"Well, I don't know about you guys," Haley said. She glanced at the clock above their heads. "But I've got to get to school."

The others nodded, and the conversation ended. They hurried toward the exit to meet their rides to school. Martina usually carpooled with Nikki and Amber to Grandview Middle School. Tori and Haley rode together to their private school, Kent Academy.

Martina was the only ninth grader in the bunch. Tori and Nikki were in the eighth grade, Haley in the seventh. And Amber, the youngest of the group, was in sixth grade.

They'd just reached the exit when a loud voice called out after them, "Wait! Don't go!"

The girls turned. Blake Michaels was waving at them. He smoothed back his dark hair as he ran to catch up with them. "Hold on!" he called out.

Martina glanced outside and saw Nikki's mother waiting for them in the Simons' red Toyota. She turned back to Blake. He had a huge smile on his face, showing off two rows of perfectly straight, white teeth. Boy, he *is* really cute, Martina thought.

Many of the girls in Silver Blades—especially Tori—had serious crushes on Blake.

Blake got right to the point. "The studio's casting department just called about the Luci Ramirez movie," he said excitedly. His smile grew even wider. "And I have terrific news!"

2

"**M**artina, you got the part!" Blake cried.

"The part?" Martina asked, not fully understanding what he meant.

"The part! In the *movie*! You were chosen as the skating double for actress Vanessa Guzman!"

"I . . . I was?" Martina said slowly.

Blake threw his arm around Martina and grinned at the other girls. "An actress named Vanessa Guzman was cast to play the part of Luci Ramirez. And you, Martina Nemo, will be doubling for her, skating the lead role!"

Martina felt a chill run through her body. Was this for real? Maybe she hadn't heard correctly. "Are you sure?" she asked nervously.

Before Blake could answer, Tori stepped forward. "What about the other skating role?" she demanded. "Did I—Who got that role?"

"Andie Levine," Blake replied. "She'll be the skating double for the actress who plays Russian skater Lydia Turnokova."

"Andie Levine!" Tori exclaimed. "Are you *joking*? She can't even do a double axel!"

While Tori let everyone know just how she felt about Andie Levine, Martina stood in complete shock. It wasn't until Nikki, Haley, and Amber began jumping up and down wildly that it began to sink in.

"This is so incredible!" Nikki shouted. She threw her arms around Martina and hugged her. "You're going to be famous!"

"I can just see your name in lights now!" Haley exclaimed. " 'Starring Seneca Hills' very own ice-skating superstar, Martina Nemo!' "

"Wow! The starring role!" Amber sighed dreamily.

"Hardly," Tori scoffed.

The girls all stopped talking and stared at Tori. She was clearly annoyed. She shifted her weight from one foot to the other and nervously played with the strap of her skating bag.

"Well, anyway," Blake said, "congratulations, Martina. We're all very pleased you were chosen. And I'm looking forward to working with you on the choreography. So what do you say we meet tomorrow morning and get started? The production company will be here tonight to set up. They'll be ready to start tomorrow."

"Wow!" Amber said again.

"The shooting schedule will be real tough," Blake went on. "It's ten long days of filming. I'll have to arrange with your parents and teachers to get you a private tutor for a week."

"Wow!" Amber said for the third time.

Martina knew everyone was staring at her, but she still couldn't find her voice. Was this really happening? For weeks she'd dreamed of being chosen, but now that it had actually happened, she was stunned. Imagine— doubling for the star of the film!

Tori's voice interrupted her thoughts. "What I meant before," she said, twirling a lock of her long blond hair around her finger, "was that while this is a great opportunity for you, Martina, just remember that Vanessa Guzman is the real star. You're only her stand-in. But anyway, I'm really happy for you." Then she nudged Haley. "Haley, come on. My mother is waiting."

Haley grinned at Martina, gave her a thumbs-up sign, then followed Tori out to Mrs. Carsen's car.

Martina, Nikki, and Amber stared after them. Nikki waited until they were out of earshot. "She didn't mean that, Tee," Nikki said.

"Yeah," Amber added, "you know Tori!"

Nikki punched Martina playfully on the shoulder. "Hey, Tee, are you just going to stand there like a mummy all day? Or are you going to say something?"

Martina gazed back at her friend in confusion. Then she remembered—she was going to be in a movie! Her face lit up. "I'm . . . I'm dreaming, right?" she asked.

Nikki and Amber both laughed. "Nope! It's no dream," Nikki assured her. "We were all here. We all heard it."

Suddenly Martina couldn't stop smiling. She felt like stopping every person she saw and shouting, "I got the part! I got the part!" Instead, she dug a quarter from her jeans pocket and dropped her skating bag on the floor.

"Ask your mom to wait a minute, okay, Nikki? I'll be right back." Then she raced to the pay phone and punched in a number quickly. She knew her mother was at work by now, but her father would be home.

When Mr. Nemo picked up, Martina could barely contain herself.

"Dad!" she shouted happily. "I'm going to be in a movie!"

3

"**I**s it true?" Cindy Adams, a ninth grader from Martina's English class, asked that afternoon. "Is it true you're going to star in a movie?"

Martina and Nikki were chatting in front of Martina's school locker. Suddenly a crowd of kids gathered around them.

Martina felt her face get hot as she tried not to blush. She couldn't believe how much attention she was getting because of this movie thing. Word about her being cast in the movie had already spread through the school.

"Well, it's true that I'm going to be in a movie," Martina replied. "But I'm not the star, that's for sure!"

She explained to her schoolmates that she was cast in a made-for-television movie about the life of Luci Ramirez. A real Hollywood actress, Vanessa Guzman, was actually playing the part of Luci. But since Vanessa couldn't skate, Martina told them, the movie producers had cast *her* to do the skating scenes.

"Wow," Cindy gushed. "Vanessa Guzman is a big star! Do you get to meet her?" The other kids stared eagerly at Martina.

"I guess," she replied. She was pretty sure she'd get to meet the young actress, since they would most likely be on the movie set at the same time.

Martina was pretty excited about meeting Vanessa Guzman. Vanessa was hugely popular. She played Mackenzie Phipps, a rich, stuck-up teenager, on Martina's favorite TV show, *Hollywood High*.

"That's so cool," Cindy sighed. "Can you get me her autograph?"

Martina laughed. "Sure. If I meet her, that is."

The bell rang, and the crowd of kids began to scatter. Nikki grabbed Martina's arm and pulled her down the hall. She leaned in close to her friend and giggled. "Can I have *your* autograph?" Nikki joked.

Martina pretended she was a famous Hollywood actress. She put on her sunglasses and faked blowing kisses and waving to invisible fans. "Of course, dahling!" Martina said in a phony accent. "Anything for my fans!"

Later that afternoon, Martina tried to work out the ache in her calf muscle. A dull pain was shooting up her left leg. It hurt just enough to stop her from practicing a sit spin properly. This was crazy! She couldn't believe that she couldn't do such an easy spin!

Glancing up, she saw Nikki, Amber, and Haley skating toward her.

"How's the star?" Haley asked with a grin.

Martina grimaced. "Some star," she muttered. "I pulled a muscle in my leg. I'm having trouble doing a simple sit spin."

Amber bent down to look at Martina's leg. She poked at it a few times. Then she gave it a quick rub. "How's that?" she asked when she finished.

Martina's eyes widened. "That actually feels better! How'd you do that?"

Amber smiled. "It's a secret," she replied. "Actually, a physical therapist showed it to me."

Martina sighed. "Well, thanks. It feels a lot better. But I'll bet there's no secret remedy to help me with my other problem."

"What's up?" Nikki asked, concerned.

Martina frowned. "Oh, nothing," she replied sarcastically. "Just my skating—it stinks! I haven't done anything right for the past two hours. Not one single move! I'm like a rag doll on ice. I can't even do my layback spin without wobbling."

"What are you talking about, Martina?" Haley asked. "You did one just this morning. And perfectly, too."

Martina shook her head. "I wish it were perfect," she groaned. "Crummy is more like it. I don't know how I managed to get cast in this movie. I'm not even *half* as good as the other skaters in Silver Blades."

Nikki stood with her hands on her hips. "Tee! Don't

say that! Of course you're as good. If you weren't, you would never have made Silver Blades in the first place!"

Martina didn't answer.

"Look, you're just nervous about this movie thing, that's all," Nikki said. "But once you get into it, it will be so much fun, you'll forget about being nervous."

"You think?" Martina asked hopefully.

"Definitely," Nikki assured her.

"Absolutely," Amber agreed.

"And anyway," Nikki went on, "Blake thinks you're perfect for the part. He said so himself. And he should know—he's choreographing the whole movie."

"I guess," Martina replied, but she wasn't convinced. All she knew was that all through afternoon practice, she'd been a mess on ice.

"Come on, let's go change," Nikki suggested.

Martina followed her friends to the locker room. Inside, Tori had already changed into a denim skirt and white T-shirt. She was brushing her hair. She mumbled hello as the others walked in.

"Hey, there's Andie Levine!" Nikki said excitedly. She called out to a pretty redheaded girl across the locker room. "Hi, Andie! Congrats about the movie!"

"Thanks," Andie called back cheerfully. "And to you too, Martina! I'm so excited! Aren't you?"

Martina felt slightly uncomfortable talking about the movie in front of the others. She didn't want to brag or anything, but she couldn't hide her excitement *all* the time.

"Definitely!" she called back to Andie. "Hey, maybe we can do lunch together during breaks." She said "do lunch" in a snobby voice, and the other girls all laughed. Except for Tori. Martina noticed that Tori rolled her eyes.

Andie waved as she left the dressing room. Martina was glad they'd be working together. Andie was skating the role of Lydia Turnokova—the famous Russian skater who had been Luci Ramirez's biggest rival. Andie was older than Martina and in the eleventh grade. They didn't hang out together or anything, but they always waved when they saw each other. Martina thought Andie was nice.

Maybe when the movie is finished, Martina thought, we'll have become better friends.

Martina took her time changing, stretching her back muscles as she moved. She hoped she wouldn't be too sore for her first day on the set the next day. Amber, Haley, and Nikki changed, too, while Tori stood over them impatiently.

"Andie seems nice," Nikki remarked after Andie and her friends left the locker room.

Martina nodded. "Yeah, she does."

Tori snickered. "I think she's totally stuck up," she said. "You should have heard her bragging during practice today about getting the part. I wanted to throw up."

"She wasn't bragging, Tori," Haley pointed out. "Everyone was asking her questions—what was she supposed to do, not answer them?"

Tori shrugged, then spun around to face the mirror again. She struck a skating pose, then sighed. "I just don't understand how *she* could have been chosen and not me."

Haley put her arm around Tori. "C'mon, Tori. Cheer up. Forget about Andie already, will you?"

Martina felt uncomfortable again. She had a sneaking suspicion the "she" Tori meant wasn't Andie Levine at all.

"Just because she looks more like Lydia doesn't mean she can skate as well." Tori was still complaining. "I can't believe the director cast on looks alone!" With that, she shot a glance at Martina.

Martina felt her face turning red. "What's that supposed to mean?"

Tori avoided Martina's gaze. "I mean, it's *obvious* why the director chose you," she replied. "He probably didn't even watch your audition tape. He probably just saw a picture of you."

"Tori!" Haley exclaimed.

"Well, it's true!" Tori shot back.

"No, it isn't!" Nikki said. "Martina is an excellent skater. She didn't get the part just because of her looks!"

"Is that what you really think?" Martina asked Tori. She had a sick feeling in the pit of stomach—a feeling that Tori might be right.

But Tori didn't answer. She flew out of the locker room, heading for the parking lot.

Haley stared after her, then picked up her bag. "Listen, Martina, forget about Tori," she said gently. "She's just jealous of you. You know how Tori's mom can be. She's probably giving Tori a hard time about not being cast in the movie. Just give Tori some time. She didn't mean it. We all know you got the part because you're a great skater."

"Tori was totally out of line," Nikki agreed.

"Not totally," Martina said. "I mean, I'm not stupid— I know there weren't loads of Hispanic skaters for the director to choose from." And though she didn't admit it out loud, Martina also knew that she wasn't nearly as good a skater as Tori or Amber. She didn't have their advanced moves.

"But *you're* the one they picked!" Nikki reminded her.

Martina ran her fingers through her hair. "I know, I know," she said. "Anyway, I have to go. My father is picking me up today, so I don't need a ride. Tell your mom, okay, Nikki?"

"Sure thing. Call me later?"

Martina nodded. "Bye, you guys. See you tomorrow," she added, flashing a smile.

Mr. Nemo was waiting in the lobby for Martina. When he saw her, he folded her into his arms. "Hey! Tina, we're so proud of you! Imagine, two actors in the family!"

"I'm hardly an actor, Dad," Martina protested.

"You're in a movie. So you're an actor!" he insisted. "And anyway, I like the way it sounds . . . my daughter, the ice actress."

"Oh, Dad, *really*!"

"I'm sure you'll be fantastic," Mr. Nemo said excitedly. "Now, come on, I have a surprise for you!"

Martina narrowed her eyes as she followed him outside. "What are you up to?" she asked suspiciously.

The surprise was in the parking lot. Martina's family was waiting for her in the minivan.

"Three cheers for Tina!" they yelled when they saw her.

Martina couldn't believe they all had come to pick her up. Her younger sister, Gabriella, Richard, and four-year-old Javier, and the baby in his car seat, were in the van. But what surprised her most was that her mom was in the front seat.

Martina hardly ever saw her mother this early in the evening. Mrs. Nemo was an attorney for a big law firm and usually worked until late at night.

"Mom! Wow! What are you doing here?"

"I took the afternoon off as soon as I heard the news!" her mother said. "We're taking you out to dinner to celebrate!"

Martina smiled as she slid in next to Gabriella.

Gabriella threw her arms around her. "You're going to be a *movie star!*" she said happily.

Martina grinned. She and her nine-year-old sister were very close. Gabriella was a skater, too. She'd skated in the last Special Olympics and had won a gold medal. The *Grandview Gazette* had run a story about Gabriella, praising her for being the only medal-winner with Down syndrome from the state of Pennsylvania.

Mr. Nemo pulled out of the parking lot and drove into town. Martina's excitement began to fade. She couldn't stop thinking about what Tori had said in the locker room. Did the others think that Martina had been chosen for the part based on her looks—and not on her skating ability?

A huge knot formed in Martina's stomach. It was still there when the family van pulled into the parking lot at Paradise Cheeseburger.

Mr. Nemo winked at Martina. "Here we are!" he said. "Your favorite restaurant!"

Martina managed a smile. She didn't want to disappoint her family. But the last thing she wanted right at that moment was a big celebration.

4

Martina laughed so hard her sides hurt. She threw a pillow at her brother. "Stop it, Richard!" she begged. "I can't breathe!"

The rest of her family was laughing, too. They had just gotten home from Paradise Cheeseburger and were sitting around the living room, helping Mr. Nemo run his lines for *Grease*.

Richard was playing the part of a car mechanic. He stood on a chair and improvised the mechanic's lines— but in the voice of a Shakespearean actor.

"Oh, woe is me!" Richard said in a stuffy British accent. He pretended to draw a sword. "Alas! But I cannot rewire this transmission!"

"My turn!" Javier cried eagerly. Javier was playing the part of a high-school football player. But since he was too young to read, Martina's mother was helping him out.

Mrs. Nemo whispered something in Javier's ear, and Javier puffed out his chest. "Can I have a monster cheese sandwich?" he said proudly.

"You dork!" Richard said, ruffling his younger brother's hair. "It's *Muenster* cheese, not *monster* cheese!"

Javier looked confused.

"That's okay, Javier," Martina said. "Richard messed up like that lots of times when he was your age. He used to think the Pledge of Allegiance said 'for Richard stands' instead of 'for which it stands.' "

Javier grinned.

Martina was feeling a lot better. They had celebrated her getting the role as if it were her birthday. Her mother had brought out a cake with skates and a movie camera drawn in blue icing. The words WAY TO GO, TINA! were written on top.

Then Nikki, Amber, and Haley had shown up at the restaurant. Martina had been so surprised to see them. Haley had said that Tori wasn't there because she had a stomachache, but Martina wasn't so sure that was the real reason.

Martina forgot about Tori as she watched her father read his lines. She was so proud of him. He was such a good actor. And all her friends kept telling her how handsome he was.

Gabriella stood up and read her part as a diner waitress. Then the scene was over. Martina checked her watch. It wasn't late, but she wanted to get to sleep early. She had to wake up at four-thirty in the morning for her first rehearsal with Blake.

She jumped up from the sofa. But before she could

say good night, her father stopped her. "Wait, Tina. You can't go to bed yet. We have something for you."

Martina grinned. "Another surprise?"

Mr. Nemo didn't answer. Instead, he dashed off to the den. He came back a second later with a wrapped package. He handed it to Martina.

"What is it?" Martina asked.

"It's a skating movie!" Gabriella said gleefully, blowing the surprise.

Mr. and Mrs. Nemo laughed. "Well, sort of," Mr. Nemo admitted. "Go ahead, honey. Open it."

Martina tore open the wrapping paper. It *was* a videocassette. She stared at the cover for a second.

"This tape has Luci Ramirez's gold-medal performance!" she shrieked.

Martina forgot all about going to sleep. She popped the cassette into the VCR, then sat down eagerly on the sofa to watch. Her family gathered around her.

She fast-forwarded the tape until she got to the ladies' figure-skating competition. Then she forwarded it some more, until it was Luci's turn to skate. Martina's heart was thumping like crazy.

Watching the tape reminded Martina of how pretty and graceful Luci Ramirez was. If Luci had been nervous, she hadn't shown it at all.

Martina sat on the edge of her seat during the entire performance. Luci was amazing! She had hit every move precisely and smiled the whole time.

"So, Tina," Richard said as the next skater took the ice. "Are those moves really hard?"

Martina thought a second before answering. "The

choreography isn't all that complicated," she said. "I think I can even do most of it pretty well. Except for the double axel. Sometimes I hit it great, but—" She turned to her parents with a panic-stricken look. "How am I going to pull off skating Luci's programs without being able to do all the moves?"

Mr. Nemo raised one eyebrow. "You'll have to ask the director about that. But they may be able to fill in parts of the routine for you."

"I want to watch Luci again," Gabriella declared.

"So do I," Martina said.

Martina became lost in Luci's performance. As soon as the tape was over, she rewound it and watched it again. Then she watched it a fourth time. She tried to memorize Luci's routine step by step. In her mind she pictured herself on the ice, skating the same routine.

"Already becoming one with your character, Tina?" her father asked.

Martina didn't take her eyes off the TV screen. "Huh?" she asked.

"Becoming one with your character," her father repeated. "It's the first rule of acting. You have to feel yourself in the role as if you really are the character, not someone playing the character. All the pros do it," he went on. "It takes a whole lot of concentration, and . . ."

But Martina was only half listening. She was too busy watching Luci Ramirez. She hoped to be just as good someday. Luci Ramirez didn't compete anymore. Instead, she toured with the Ice Capades. Luci was known as the Queen of the Ice Capades.

Martina grinned. Maybe she would follow in Luci's footsteps. Maybe Martina would become the next Queen of the Ice Capades!

Richard's voice interrupted her thoughts. "It's weird, Tina, but if you wore your hair back like that, you'd look just like Luci."

Mr. Nemo turned to stare at his daughter. "You know, your brother is right. You do look an awful lot like her."

Gabriella and Mrs. Nemo nodded in agreement.

Martina smoothed her hair back and got up to look in the den mirror. She stared at her reflection. They were right! She *did* look like a young Luci Ramirez.

Suddenly that knot in her stomach returned and Tori's voice ran through her head: "It's obvious why the director chose you!"

Martina silently willed the knot to go away. So maybe the director *did* choose me because I look like Luci Ramirez, she thought. But I can skate like her, too!

And whatever it takes, I'm going to skate my best in this movie and show Tori—and everyone else—that Martina Nemo is perfect for this part!

5

At five the next morning the Nemos' minivan turned into the entrance of the Seneca Hills Ice Arena. Martina sat in the front next to her father. Nikki, Haley, and Amber sat behind them in the middle seat. Tori had called Martina early that morning to say she didn't need a ride to the rink because her mother was driving her.

Yeah, right, Martina had thought. Another lame excuse.

The minivan drove at a snail's pace along the wooded road toward the parking lot.

"What's with all this traffic on a Saturday morning?" Martina asked. She edged forward in her seat to get a better look. All she could see ahead of them was a line of cars slowly turning into the parking lot.

"I've never seen it so crowded," Nikki said.

The girls all leaned forward to stare out the windshield. As they neared the parking lot they finally saw the reason for all the traffic. Four huge trucks were parked out in front of the Ice Arena, blocking the lot. Written in huge letters across each truck was MOBILE STAR PRODUCTIONS. Across from the trucks were three large trailers.

"Wow!" Amber said excitedly. "This is all for the movie!"

Martina gasped in amazement. Dozens of people were bustling about, unloading cameras, lights, and sound equipment. This was so incredibly exciting!

Mr. Nemo couldn't pull any closer to the building. "I guess this is where you girls get out," he said. "Have a great practice. And Tina," he added, winking at his daughter, "knock 'em dead!"

Martina returned her father's wink and shut the door to the van. She walked with her friends toward the Arena. She felt stunned by all the commotion.

"Look at all these people!" Haley let out a whistle. "I can't believe how many people it takes to make one little movie!"

"Incredible," Nikki remarked. "And look at those big trailers. I'll bet those are for the movie stars."

Martina's eyes widened. "You think Vanessa Guzman is in one of those trailers?" she asked.

Nikki nodded. "Definitely."

A strange, mischievous smile crept across Haley's face. "Let's go check it out, then!" she said. She headed toward one of the trailers.

"Don't stars have bodyguards or something?" Amber asked, pulling her back.

"So what?" Haley replied. "We'll just say we're with Martina. She *is* in the movie, after all."

Martina bit her bottom lip. She was sure that mentioning her name wouldn't impress the bodyguards in the least. "I don't know . . . ," she said uneasily.

"Oh, don't worry, Martina," Haley said. She pulled her friend by the arm. "Come on. It's worth a try, isn't it?"

Martina gave a reluctant shrug. "I guess."

They walked toward the trailers and pushed through the crowd of kids who were standing around, gawking. The kids were all either members of Silver Blades or of the Seneca Hills Hawks ice-hockey team. Both the Silver Blades club and the Hawks practiced at the rink every morning and afternoon.

Suddenly a door to one of the trailers opened and a pretty girl of about sixteen emerged. Martina and her friends recognized her immediately.

"Vanessa Guzman!" Nikki cried.

Vanessa climbed down the few steps from her trailer door to the ground. She wore a short black dress under a faded denim jacket, and black high-top sneakers. Dark sunglasses covered her eyes. Her short, jet-black hair was parted on the side and slicked back. Martina and her friends stared at the young star, their mouths hanging open.

"She looks so cool!" Nikki whispered to Martina.

Martina nodded. "I love her dress," she whispered back.

"You ought to wear your hair that way," Haley said to Martina.

"You'd look awesome like that!" Amber agreed.

Martina's fingers ran through her hair. She'd always wanted to do something more dramatic with her hair, but she never knew what. She usually wore it hanging down or pushed behind her ears. Sometimes she stuck a barrette in just for a change. She decided she was definitely going to try wearing it slicked back like Vanessa's.

"She looks much prettier in person than on *Hollywood High*," Martina remarked.

"Let's introduce ourselves," Haley said. "It doesn't seem like she has any bodyguards."

Martina nodded. She was a little nervous, but excited just the same.

Vanessa was already busy signing autographs for some of the Silver Blades kids. Martina, Nikki, Haley, and Amber pushed their way toward her.

"Vanessa! Hey, Vanessa!" Haley called out.

Vanessa looked up and smiled at them. Martina thought her smile seemed genuine. She seemed to be enjoying all the attention.

"Would you guys like autographs, too?" Vanessa asked.

Haley's eyes lit up. "Sure!" she said, rummaging through her skating bag for something for Vanessa to sign.

"Would you sign my autograph book?" Amber asked shyly. She pulled a small padlike book with a lot of blank pages from her bag. She smiled sheepishly at the other girls. "I always carry it with me," she explained. "Just in case."

Vanessa took the book and signed her name. Amber stared at the signature and smiled. "Now I have two celebrity autographs. One from Trisha McCoy and one from Vanessa!" Trisha McCoy was a famous ice skater. Amber had met her when she had skated in the *Nutcracker on Ice* Christmas show that winter.

"Can I sign something for you?" Vanessa asked, looking at Martina.

Martina turned red instantly. She couldn't believe how nervous she felt around the TV star.

Nikki pushed Martina forward. "Martina is going to be in the movie with you!" she said proudly.

Vanessa took off her sunglasses and looked at the girls in confusion.

"She's your skating double!" Haley added.

Vanessa still seemed confused. Then suddenly her face brightened. "Oh, right!" she said. "I saw your videotaped routine. You're really an excellent skater, Martina."

Martina grinned from ear to ear. She was being praised by a big star! "Thanks," she replied. "And you're an excellent actress, too," she added. It seemed polite to praise Vanessa as well. "We all love *Hollywood High.*"

"What's Marcus Miller really like?" Amber asked dreamily. Marcus Miller was one of the most adorable actors on the show.

Vanessa laughed. "He's really sweet," she told them. "And an amazing kisser."

"Wow!" Amber said.

Just then Vanessa waved to someone behind them.

They all spun around to see an older girl with red hair standing in the doorway of another trailer.

"Hi, Jordana!" Vanessa called out. "That's Jordana Moore," she told the girls. "She's in the movie, too. She's playing Lydia Turnokova."

"Our friend Andie is skating for her," Martina said.

Vanessa smiled at them. "Well, I'd better get going now," she said. "It was nice meeting you all. I'm sure I'll see you on the set, Miranda."

"Uh, it's Martina," Martina corrected her.

Vanessa covered her mouth. "Oops! I'm sorry!" she apologized. Then she moved through the crowd and up the steps into Jordana Moore's trailer. When the door closed behind her, the crowd of kids began to filter into the rink.

"Hey, there's Tori!" Nikki said. "Wait till she hears we met Vanessa Guzman!"

"Why didn't she ride with us today?" Amber asked Martina.

"She said it was because her mother wanted to drive her," Martina explained.

"Well, come on, let's go tell her about Vanessa!" Nikki said.

Martina followed them over to Tori. But she would have much rather just gone straight into the Ice Arena. She felt nervous around Tori. She and Tori had never been close. Martina never felt that Tori had fully accepted her into their group. If Tori was supposed to be Martina's friend, like everyone said, then why had Tori been so mean to her the day before in the locker room?

Haley had said Tori was just having a bad day, but still . . .

"Hey, Tori," Nikki said. "Guess who we just met?"

Tori looked bored. "Yeah, I know, Vanessa Guzman. I saw you guys talking to her. Big deal."

Amber's eyes widened. "What are you talking about?" she asked. "Vanessa is on TV! She's kissed Marcus Miller!"

Tori shrugged. "Well, I think this whole movie thing is totally out of control. A big disruption. I mean, it's already five-thirty and practice hasn't even started yet. Everybody's so obsessed with the movie—like they've never seen famous people before. How long are we going to have to wait to use the rink, anyway? I didn't wake up early today just to sit around and stare at dumb movie equipment."

Martina had a feeling that Tori was having *another* bad day.

"Really, Tori," Haley said, "it's not as terrible as you're making it out to be."

"Well," Tori said, "is it going to be like this for the next ten days? Why do we have to share a rink with the Hawks while the movie gets a whole rink for itself? I mean, what's more important, Silver Blades or a stupid movie?"

Martina was beginning to get annoyed. Why was Tori making such a big deal? It was only for ten days.

"And did you see Andie Levine?" Tori went on. "Parading around like she's some star or something? I mean, she's only a skating double in a dumb TV movie.

I think she's a terrible skater, anyway. She'll probably mess up her first scene."

Before Martina could open her mouth to argue, Haley spoke up loudly. "So, Martina, we'd better get going to practice. Have fun at rehearsal! And say hi to Blake for us!" She winked at Martina, and Martina managed a small smile.

"Can you meet us for lunch at the snack bar?" Nikki asked. "And tell us everything about the movie?"

Martina avoided looking at Tori's scowling face as she answered. "Sure," she replied, walking toward the other rink. "See you later."

"You know what they say in show biz," Tori called out.

"What?" Martina asked.

"Break a leg!" The other girls just stared at Tori. "Come on, you guys, it was a *joke*!" Tori insisted.

Martina tried to smile, but deep down she didn't believe Tori meant it as a joke at all.

6

"It feels weird out here with no one from Silver Blades skating," Martina said. She and Blake had the ice to themselves. Around them, movie crew members worked busily. Some put scenery walls up, some moved cables around, and others adjusted lights. Martina watched them excitedly out of the corner of her eye as she listened to Blake.

"When a movie is made, scenes are filmed in bits and pieces. Then they are put together in order at the very end," Blake explained to her. "So don't be confused by the sequence in which your scenes will be shot. As a matter of fact, one of the first scenes the director wants to shoot is Luci's gold-medal performance."

Martina's eyes lit up. "The *Pirates of Penzance* number?" she asked.

Blake smiled. "You've been doing your homework."

Martina nodded enthusiastically. "I pretty much know the whole thing by heart already," she said. "My parents gave me a tape of the routine. I watched it all night last night!"

Blake seemed impressed. "Good for you. So you know there's nothing too complicated in the routine. Except Luci's signature move, the Ramirez spiral."

Martina winced at the words. No way could she do the Ramirez spiral. It was an unassisted death spiral. That was usually a pairs move, with the boy holding the girl's hand while the girl stretched out her body in a straight horizontal line. The girl had to be as close to the ice as possible as she spun around and around.

A singles skater performed an unassisted death spiral by bending very far backward, all on her own, with no one to hold her hand. The layback spin was the most similar move for a singles skater. And Martina's layback spin was excellent. But it was a long way from a layback spin to an unassisted death spiral.

"Don't worry, Martina," Blake said. "This is the movie business, remember? You won't have to perform the move exactly. You just do the best you can, and we'll work a little movie magic around it."

"Really?" Martina asked. "That's cool. So it will look like I did it, right?"

Blake nodded.

Martina grinned. She wouldn't tell anybody about the movie magic until after they saw the movie. She couldn't wait to see their faces as they watched her do an unassisted death spiral!

Martina stepped onto the ice and waited for Blake to push a button on a tiny tape recorder. The music from *Pirates* came blaring out, and Blake joined her on the ice. He started to skate the routine, with Martina following close behind.

"Excellent!" Blake said. "You weren't kidding about having the routine almost memorized."

"Well, I watched it on tape at least twenty times last night!" Martina replied.

Blake and Martina worked all morning on the *Pirates* number. Martina was surprised at how easily it came. As she skated she imagined she was at the Olympics. She convinced herself that each move was do-or-die. She got into it so completely that she hit each jump and turn with just the right timing and energy.

It was nearly time for lunch when Martina skated the number on her own. When her final sit spin slowed to a stop, she glanced up to see Blake frowning at her.

"Almost!" he said. "Now let's take that last spin one more time, more slowly. See if you can hold it longer."

Blake was showing Martina where to position her arms when she heard loud voices at the other end of the rink. She saw her friends waving to her from the entrance.

"Can I take a quick break?" Martina asked.

Blake nodded, and Martina skated over. A movie production assistant was blocking Tori, Nikki, Amber, and Haley from coming into the rink.

"What do you mean, we can't come in?" Tori demanded. "You can't keep us out of *our* club's rink! We have a right to be here! We're in Silver Blades!"

"I'm sorry, miss," the production assistant told her. "There's a rehearsal for the film going on in here, and—"

"I don't care!" Tori insisted. "See the name on the banner over there? It says 'Silver Blades.'" She turned around so the production assistant could see the back of her jacket. "And see what my jacket says? Silver Blades."

"Miss, I'm sorry, but I can't let you in."

"Can I talk to them for a sec?" Martina asked politely. "This is all my fault. I told them to come by to get me around lunchtime."

The production assistant glanced at Martina.

"She's the star we told you about," Nikki told him. "We know her personally."

Martina's face reddened.

"She's not a star," the production assistant said. "I've never seen her before."

Martina felt very small. "Uh, I'm in the movie," she explained softly. She showed him her stage pass. "See?"

The production assistant examined her pass, then nodded. "Yeah, okay. But I can't let them in. It's the director's rules. You'll have to step out of the rink if you want to see them."

Martina left the rink, totally embarrassed by the tight security. "Uh, hi, guys," she said.

"Hey, Tee!" Nikki said. "I can't believe we had trouble trying to meet you for lunch."

"Yeah, your *bodyguard* wouldn't let us in!" Tori joked.

"He's not my bodyguard," Martina explained. "He works for the production company. But I don't think I can go with you to the snack bar."

"Oh, come on," Haley said. "We want to hear all—"

"I'm sorry, really, but I don't think I even get a break for lunch today. After my session with Blake, I have to be fitted for costumes, then get my makeup done, then—"

Tori made a face. "Forget it, guys. We've lost Martina. She's already gone Hollywood on us!"

Martina's chest tightened. "I didn't mean to sound like that," she tried to explain. "It's just—I don't— There isn't—"

"It's no big deal, Martina," Tori said. "We understand. Maybe next time. Come on, you guys," she said to the others. "We don't have much more time for lunch."

"Maybe we'll see you later?" Nikki asked hopefully.

"Definitely!" Martina said. "After rehearsal, I promise! I'll catch up with you over at Super Sundaes."

"Great," Nikki said. "We'll meet you there at five-thirty."

"See you then," Tori said. She turned to Haley, Amber, and Nikki. "You won't believe the cute new guy on the Hawks. I think he's in the snack bar now. Let's go!"

Martina felt a little pang as her friends walked away. She watched as they all giggled and gossiped.

Martina sighed and headed back to Blake. Here she was, making a movie. She was supposed to be the envy of all. Yet she envied her friends. They were having so much fun together. Who would have thought that making a movie would be so boring?

7

Martina stood perfectly still on top of a chair. She felt completely ridiculous wrapped in yards of bright green fabric. Kirsten Costello, the costume designer, was taking her measurements for the four costumes Martina had to wear in the movie.

"Can I put my arm down now?" Martina asked hopefully. Her shoulder was already aching from holding her arm up, Statue of Liberty style, as she was measured.

"In a sec," Kirsten replied through a mouthful of pins.

Martina sighed, then craned her neck to check the clock above the door. It was after five-thirty. She groaned. There was no way she was going to make it to Super Sundaes, as she'd promised. She could just imagine Tori's reaction when she didn't show up. She'd have a big smirk across her face, telling the others, "I *told* you she wouldn't show."

Martina sighed again, then was finally told she was finished. She climbed down from the chair and stretched her shoulder muscles. She grabbed her things and ran back to the rink to meet Blake.

Blake *was* extremely good-looking, and Martina knew any girl in Silver Blades would kill to spend all day with him. But after seven hours with the choreographer, she was actually tired of him. They had practiced until one, then Martina had been allowed to grab a quick bite for lunch.

Afterward they had resumed practice until four. Then she'd been whisked away to see Kirsten. And now she was facing more practice with Blake. Martina was used to waking up early. She was used to long skating days for Silver Blades. But this movie schedule was something else!

Blake waved her over and began showing her more of the routine. Nearby, some of the crew members were having a heated discussion about where to put a spotlight. Martina listened, wondering if the spotlight was for her.

"Hello? Martina?" Blake asked in annoyance. "Come on! Pay attention!"

Martina gulped. "Sorry, Blake." She tried to stifle a yawn. But she was feeling really bored. She just couldn't understand why Blake was making her do the routine over and over when she already knew it.

Across the rink, Martina caught Andie Levine's eye. Andie was working on her routines with Cori Lerner,

Blake's new assistant choreographer. Andie pretended to wipe her brow in exhaustion as she made a face at Martina. Martina laughed out loud. Obviously Andie was having a grueling day, too.

"What's so funny, Martina?" Blake demanded.

"Oh, nothing," Martina replied. "Uh, Blake, what time will we be finished this afternoon?" she asked. "I want to call my father and let him know when to come get me."

Blake shrugged. "I'm not sure," he answered. "But what I *am* sure of is that it won't be this *afternoon*. It'll be more like this *evening*."

"This evening?" Martina echoed. "But I'm beat!"

"The lighting director wants to run through the scene," Blake explained. "You won't have to skate it for him. He just wants to check your positioning."

"What about Jake Collins?" Martina asked. Jake Collins was the film's director. "I haven't even met him yet."

Blake chuckled. "Oh, you'll meet him," he replied. "First thing tomorrow morning, when we work on this scene!"

Martina whirled around and stared at Blake in shock. "Tomorrow? So soon? Seriously?"

Blake nodded.

Wow, Martina thought. I'd better pay attention. And she didn't take her eyes off Blake for the rest of the evening, except when she took a break to call first her father, to tell him what time to pick her up, and then Nikki, to apologize for not showing up at Super Sundaes.

"It's okay," Nikki told her. "We all understand."

"Even Tori?" Martina asked. She felt a little uncomfortable asking, since Nikki and Tori were good friends.

Nikki hesitated. "Well, Tori did make a few jokes about your having a star complex, but we all let her have it."

"You did?"

"Yup! We told her to stop teasing you already. Haley even told her to stop acting jealous!"

"Haley said that?"

"Uh-huh."

Martina smiled. "Thanks, you guys."

"Don't mention it. Tori's always like this, Tee. She's really upset about losing out to Andie Levine. So she's acting weird and all, taking it out on you. But we're all really happy for you, Tee. Tori too. It will just take her a little longer to show it."

Martina thought about that. "Well, I'm not holding my breath," she said. "Anyway, I wish you guys could keep me company out here. It is *so* boring!"

"Really?" Nikki asked.

"Yeah. It's nothing like I thought it would be. It's sort of like Silver Blades—only more exhausting. Blake made me skate the same routine over and over all day long. When I first did it, it was so exciting. But then, after the twentieth time, I was like, okay, enough already!"

Nikki laughed.

"Oh, and then I had to walk through the routine for the lighting director—*that* was a load of laughs," she added sarcastically. "I had to stand on the ice in different skating poses so he could see which color lights looked best. You should have seen me waiting forever in the camel position while he tried to choose between a red or a blue spotlight! I looked like such a jerk!"

"Sounds grim," Nikki said sympathetically.

Martina saw Blake Michaels waving to her and groaned. "It's Blake," she told Nikki. "I've nicknamed him Sarge Two."

Nikki chuckled. The girls all called their coach, Kathy Bart, Sarge because she was as demanding as an army sergeant.

"I have to go," Martina said.

"Okay, we'll see you in the morning," Nikki said.

"What are you talking about?" Martina asked. "Tomorrow's Sunday. We don't practice on Sundays."

"Do you think we'd miss seeing you skate in your first movie scene?" Nikki asked.

"But they're filming at six A.M.!" Martina told her.

"I know," Nikki replied. "See you then!"

Martina returned to the ice and ran through her routine a few more times with Blake. Now she was glad Blake had pushed her so hard all day. She was feeling really confident with the routine. She only hoped she wouldn't forget everything by the next morning.

Blake finally told her they were finished for the day. Martina checked the time and nearly fainted.

"Nine-thirty!" she cried.

"Nice first day," Blake assured her. "You're really working hard, Martina. And doing a terrific job."

Martina gave him a tired smile, then rushed out to

meet her father. He was waiting in the minivan, singing along with the soundtrack from *Grease*.

"Hey!" he said when she got into the car. "How'd it go?"

"I'm exhausted," Martina said, slumping in the seat next to him.

"We're all so proud of you, Tina," Mr. Nemo said. "We're thrilled to have such a talented skating star in the family."

"Thanks, Dad," Martina said with a yawn. She told him all about her day during the ride home—how it had been both exciting *and* boring.

Once they got home, all Martina wanted to do was go to sleep. But she had to repeat the day's events for the rest of her family first. By the time she fell into bed, it was ten-thirty.

Martina fluffed her pillow and settled her head into the softness. She thought about what her father had said about being a star. She knew she wasn't *really* the star of the movie, but she did have a very important role.

She stretched her aching muscles one last time. Boy, her legs were killing her! Must have been all those sit spins.

She closed her eyes and fell asleep wondering how in the world she was going to wake up and be ready to skate again in just five hours.

8

Martina glanced at the clock on the dashboard. It was five A.M., but she was wide awake. She couldn't wait to get to the Arena for her first day of filming.

"Can't you drive any faster, Dad?" she asked.

Mr. Nemo laughed. "Don't worry, honey. We won't be late. There's no traffic at this hour."

Martina stared out the window. Outside, it was completely dark and quiet.

But lights blazed inside the Arena. Dozens of people bustled about getting ready for first call. *Call* was the movie term used for the time you were supposed to be on the set, ready to start. Martina's call for this morning was six A.M.

Martina stood on the side of the rink, watching. Everybody was busy. Crew members hooked up lights, moved cameras, and adjusted microphones. Others prepared scripts, checked lists, and swept. Even the

Zamboni was already at work. It trudged slowly across the rink, smoothing the ice.

Martina was surprised to see so many people on the set. She didn't know why, but she'd thought it would just be her, Blake, the director, and a few crew members to work the camera. There must be a hundred people here, she thought.

"Martina, right?" somebody said.

Martina turned to see Vanessa Guzman smiling at her. She thought Vanessa looked amazing, considering it was so early in the morning. The actress yawned, then said, "I can't believe I'm awake at this hour! I feel so . . . *blah!*"

"Me too," Martina said, though she wasn't quite sure she believed Vanessa. The young actress looked gorgeous. She was wearing a bright green skating costume. It had silver and green sequins at the collar and a mesh neckline and back. Her makeup was perfect, and her hair was slicked back the way it had been the previous day.

"Is that the costume for the *Pirates* routine?" Martina asked.

Vanessa turned slightly, modeling the outfit. "Yes, it's smashing, isn't it?" she asked.

Well, I wouldn't use that word to describe it, Martina thought to herself, but she nodded in agreement anyway.

"I guess I should go change into mine," Martina said. "Will I see you later?" she asked.

Vanessa nodded. "Maybe we can grab a soda together during the break."

"That would be great!" Martina replied.

Vanessa waved, then went over to speak to a crew member. Martina headed for the makeshift costume department, which was really a corner of the women's locker room. Andie was already there, getting fitted for her costume.

"You look fantastic," Martina told her. Andie's costume was bright red and set off the color of her hair perfectly.

Andie looked up but barely smiled.

"What's wrong?" Martina asked.

"I . . . I'm so nervous!" Andie said, her voice cracking slightly.

Martina put a hand on the older girl's shoulder. "I saw you skate yesterday," she told her. "You were great! Don't worry, you'll be fine."

"Aren't you nervous?" Andie asked anxiously.

The truth was, Martina was incredibly nervous about skating in front of everybody that morning. What if she messed up? What if the director decided he'd made a mistake in casting an amateur skater? Martina just hoped she'd be able to keep her breakfast down once she got on the ice.

"A little," she lied. "But I can't think about it. If I think about it, I'm a lost cause."

"I know what you mean," Andie said. "At least you're skating before me today."

"Right," Martina said, wishing Andie hadn't reminded her.

Martina found her costume and put it on. She turned a few times in front of the mirror to see how she looked. The costume looked terrific, that was for sure. The only problem was that the sleeves were a tiny bit snug.

Martina hurried out on the rink. She did her off-ice warm-up. After stretching, she sat on a bench to lace up her skates. Blake tapped her shoulder while she was pulling the laces tight.

"Martina Nemo, this is Jake Collins, the director."

Martina looked up immediately and smiled. "Hi. It's nice to meet you," she said.

Jake Collins smiled back at her. He was a lot younger than Martina had imagined he'd be. He wore faded jeans and a black vest over a white T-shirt. His long blond hair was pulled back in a ponytail.

"It's nice to meet you, too," Jake told her. "Blake has a lot of nice things to say about you. And I must say, your audition tape was *fabulous*."

Jake emphasized the word *fabulous*. Martina wondered if all Hollywood people used words such as *smashing* and *fabulous*.

"Thank you," she said shyly, grateful her face had turned only slightly red.

"I'm sure you're even more marvelous in person," Jake added with a wink.

Suddenly a loud sound rose from the bleachers.

Martina glanced up and was surprised to see Nikki, Haley, and Amber calling to her from the top row. They were stomping and waving furiously. Martina wondered how they had gotten past the security guards. She figured Haley had dreamed up some crazy story to get them in. Haley was a genius at that kind of thing.

Martina wanted to wave back, but Jake was standing right beside her. She couldn't believe they had all woken up so early on their day off to come watch her skate.

All except Tori, she noted.

"Your fan club?" Jake asked.

Now Martina turned totally red. She nodded.

"Well, then, I'll let them stay this time," he said. "But I'm sorry to say that for the rest of the week, this is a closed set."

"A closed set?" Martina asked.

"No outsiders allowed," Jake translated. "Now, what do you say we get started? You should know right off the bat that I'm a very punctual man. I despise tardiness. But I'm sure you won't give me any trouble."

Martina made a pact with herself right there and then to be extra early for all of her scenes. "I promise—" she started to tell Jake. But Jake was already off, talking to the sound engineer.

Before taking her position on the ice, Martina glanced up to wave at her friends. She was so glad they had come. For some reason, knowing they were there made her less nervous. Her father was somewhere up there, too. He had been eager to come watch her that morning.

Standing on the ice waiting for her cue, Martina glanced around the rink. Then she saw someone walk in and sit down near the director's chair—and her mouth fell open.

Tori!

Tori was dressed in a bright green skating costume. Her mother was with her.

Why is Tori here? Martina wondered. It's her day off. And why is she all dressed up to skate?

9

Martina didn't have a chance to think about Tori, because Blake suddenly gave her the cue to get into position. Martina took a deep breath. She skated around the ice a couple of times to warm up. She got into her starting position just as a bright spotlight flashed directly on her.

Her heart started thumping madly. Suddenly everything was all so *real*.

Martina swallowed hard. She was about to skate in a movie! She tried to forget that she was in front of movie cameras and concentrate on the routine. She reminded herself to think about Luci. Her father had told her a trillion times to become one with the character. That was what she needed to do now. Become Luci Ramirez—at least for the next few hours.

Someone called out, "All quiet on the set!" The lights were shut off. All that was lit was the spotlight—and it was focused on her. The entire rink became still and quiet.

Chill, Martina! she told herself. Or they'll hear your breathing up in the bleachers!

But as soon as the music began, Martina felt confident. Suddenly she wasn't nervous anymore. She forgot about the cameras and all the people watching her. All she thought about was the routine. She glided across the ice, soaring into her first big jump.

Things were going perfectly. Martina prepared for a double loop jump. Suddenly Jake Collins shouted, "Stop!"

Within seconds the music cut off. The lights in the rink snapped back on. People began talking and rushing around her.

Martina was dumbfounded. What had she done wrong? Had her axel not been high enough? Had she messed up a crossover? She looked over at Blake in a panic, but he was busy talking to Jake. She saw Jake nod, then say something to the lighting director. Then, all at once, the lights went back out and the spotlight came back on.

"Take it from the second set of crossovers, Martina," Blake called to her.

Martina was confused but did as he said. The music came back on, and she tried to get her bearings. Luckily, it took only a second, and soon she was back into the routine, preparing for her double loop. She skated quickly around the rink, but before she knew it, Jake again yelled, "Stop!"

Martina stopped skating. She felt the tears well up

in her eyes. The lights hadn't come back on and she was in the bright spotlight, unable to see anyone around her.

Finally Blake called to her again. "Take it from the preparation for the double loop!" he shouted.

Martina swallowed the lump in her throat and tried to concentrate. What was going on? Was she messing up big-time? She didn't have time to think about it because the music came back on and she had to skate. She did her best to focus on her skating, but she was really anxious by now.

For the next hour Martina skated and stopped, skated and stopped. Three times the director asked her to start from the very beginning. All the while she tried to catch Blake's attention, but she couldn't.

Finally she finished the number and was told to sit on the bench. At that moment Vanessa took up where Martina had left off. Vanessa ran through her next scene with Jake.

Martina sat on the same bench for the next two hours while Vanessa acted the same scene over and over, repeating her lines endlessly. Jake had the camera shoot her from four different positions. Then Vanessa had to say her lines another three times just for the sound engineer.

Martina couldn't believe how boring the whole thing was. Sure, the first few times were interesting. But hearing the lines over and over was getting kind of annoying. She'd always imagined moviemaking to be fun and exciting. Meanwhile, all she'd done since finishing her scene was sit and wait.

Finally, at noon, Jake called for lunch. Martina stood up and searched for her father. She'd arranged to meet him for lunch at the snack bar. A few minutes later he appeared with Nikki, Amber, and Haley.

"You were great!" Mr. Nemo declared proudly.

"Awesome!" Haley added.

Nikki and Amber hugged her.

Great? Awesome? Martina couldn't believe her ears. "I was terrible!" she said, very close to tears. "It was all so embarrassing!"

"What are you talking about, Tina?" her father asked. "You skated beautifully."

"Then how come the director stopped me every ten seconds?" Martina asked. "I was so humiliated! He must have used up fifty rolls of film on me alone!" The tears began to fall. It was embarrassing to cry in front of everyone, but she couldn't help it.

Just then Blake came up behind them and put his arm around Martina. "Great job, Martina!" he told her. "Hey," he said softly as he noticed her tears. "What's wrong?"

Martina wiped her eyes. "Why did Jake stop so often?" she asked, sniffling. "He must have filmed me a dozen times! What was I doing wrong?"

"Martina, the director didn't film your scene today— he blocked it," Blake told her.

"Huh?" Martina sniffed again.

"It's called blocking," Blake repeated. "It's a technical term. A director always blocks a scene before he shoots it. It's his way of recording where you'll be during the routine so he can set up the camera shot. That's why he had to stop you so often. Not because you were messing up, but because he was recording your moves. We'll film the scene for real tomorrow morning."

Martina stared at him and let it all sink in. She breathed a sigh of relief. "Really?" she asked.

Blake nodded.

"Well, that makes sense," she said. "I just wish I had known!"

"Sorry, Martina," Blake apologized. "I thought you did."

"Martina, when did your unassisted death spiral get so good?" Amber exclaimed. "You looked awesome!"

"Blake helped me with it yesterday," Martina said, smiling at the choreographer.

"Well, we'd better get some lunch," Mr. Nemo said. "I'll go get us a table."

"Luci Ramirez's routine is just great, Martina," Amber said as the girls all headed for the locker room. "You looked as though you'd been practicing it for months!"

"Not quite," Martina said, feeling more cheerful. "But at least this is the longest of the four programs I have to learn. The rest are really pretty short."

"That costume is awesome," Nikki said, reaching out to touch the shiny green material.

"Thanks," Martina said. Then she asked the question that had been nagging at her for hours. "Hey, what is Tori doing here with her mother?"

"Tori's here?" Nikki asked.

Haley squinted and looked around the Arena. "Are you sure?"

Martina nodded. "With her mother. Didn't you see them? They sat on the bottom bleacher. And Tori's in a new costume. It's green like mine, too."

"Really?" Amber asked, sounding as surprised as the others. "I didn't see them, but it's pretty crowded here this morning."

Haley suddenly nudged Martina in the ribs. "Check out Vanessa!" she whispered, pointing across the rink to the actress. Vanessa was surrounded by guys. From a distance she seemed to be flirting up a storm.

Haley reached up and fluffed her hair, imitating Vanessa. "Oh, really! You don't say!" she said in a phony sweet voice. She did such a bad impression of Vanessa that Martina had to laugh out loud.

"You laughed! See? You're feeling better already!" Haley pointed out.

Martina grinned. "I am," she replied. "But don't make fun of Vanessa so much—she's really nice."

Nikki made a face. "I don't know. There's something about her."

Amber nodded. "Yeah, like, if she's so nice, then why'd she treat Marcus Miller like dirt?"

"That was on TV, Amber!" Martina said. "She was playing the part of Mackenzie Phipps when she did that. Vanessa isn't at all snobby and mean like her character on *Hollywood High*."

Haley folded her arms across her chest. "Maybe not," she admitted. "But she's still the biggest flirt I've ever seen!" She pointed to Vanessa, who was pouffing her hair again.

The girls all laughed, Martina included.

"Come on, let's get lunch," Martina said. "I'm starving! And I have to be back on the set in"—she glanced up at the clock on the wall and groaned—"sixteen minutes!"

10

On Monday morning Mr. Nemo dropped Martina off at the Ice Arena a little before four-thirty.

"I wish I could stay to watch today," he said disappointedly. "But I have to get back to drive Javier to nursery school."

"That's okay, Dad," Martina told him. "I'll tell you all about it later."

Mr. Nemo nodded with a sad look on his face. Then he brightened. "Okay, so do you remember everything I told you?" he asked eagerly.

Martina groaned. "Yes, Dad! How could I forget? You've told me a hundred times!" She opened the door to the van and started to get out.

Mr. Nemo turned off the engine. "So let's hear it."

Martina rolled her eyes and sat back down. "Okay. To remember the three rules of acting, remember the three C's. Be *calm*. Become one with your *char-*

acter. And"—she made a face at her father—"don't *choke*!"

They both laughed.

"Excellent!" Mr. Nemo said.

Martina jumped out of the van and closed the door. She leaned in the open window and blew a kiss to her father.

"Wait!" Mr. Nemo called to her. "There's one more thing to remember. The most important thing of all."

"Now what?" Martina asked.

He handed a bag through the window. "Your skates," he said, smiling.

She bit her bottom lip. "Oh, right," she said.

Martina waved to her father as the van pulled away. Then she slung her skate bag over her shoulder and headed into the Arena. She went right to the locker room, where Kirsten was waiting for her.

"I let out your sleeves a little," Kirsten said, handing Martina the costume. "And I took it in a bit at the back."

Martina slipped the costume on and checked out her reflection.

"You look fabulous!" Kirsten said.

"Thanks," Martina said. "The changes make a huge difference." She admired herself briefly. Then she headed to the makeup department, which was really a chair and a big mirror set up next to the rink.

Gustav Petersen, the makeup man, examined Martina. He applied some cakey makeup base to her face. He outlined her eyes thickly with black eyeliner, then brushed red blush on her cheeks. Even though lots of girls in Martina's ninth-grade class wore makeup, Martina preferred going natural. It felt weird to suddenly have all this stuff on her face.

Gustav reached for a tub of gel and put a glob of it in her hair. Using a comb, he slicked it straight back—just the way Luci's had been in the video. When he finished, Martina stared at her reflection in amazement. She looked just like a young Luci Ramirez—and she loved it! She made a mental note to buy some of the same hair gel next time she was at the store.

Martina stepped out on the ice to warm up. She circled the rink a few times, then stopped to stretch her muscles. She was bent over, stretching her back, when she heard a voice.

"Hey! Martina!"

She looked up to see Vanessa leaning on the rink rail. It was funny to see them dressed alike, with identical hair and makeup. Martina felt as though she'd suddenly gotten a twin.

"So, are you ready?" Vanessa asked.

Martina nodded. "I think so," she said. "I'm a little nervous, though."

"It helps to block everything else out," Vanessa told her. "Pretend the cameras and all the people aren't there."

"Is that how you do it?" Martina asked.

Vanessa nodded. "Uh-huh. My first season with *Hollywood High* I had never been in front of cameras before, except for still cameras when I was modeling. I was so nervous! There were, like, about a million people watching me. And I was sure I would mess up. But

I pretended they weren't there. It was easy. It gets so quiet on the set when they're filming. Not like this," she added. "The rink is pretty noisy. But you'll see. Everything in the background will disappear once your scene begins."

Martina couldn't believe she was getting acting advice from a real star! Vanessa was so friendly. She was talking to Martina as though they'd known each other for years.

"Martina." The assistant director came up to them. "Time for you to take the ice."

Vanessa leaned over toward Martina and held out a small glass jar. "Here," she said. "It's special lip gloss. It won't change the color of your lip makeup, and it will keep your lips from chapping under the bright lights."

Martina stuck her fingertip in the jar and took some gloss. "Thanks!"

Vanessa waved, then left. "Good luck! See ya later!"

Martina applied the gloss to her lips. She couldn't get over how nice Vanessa was. She wondered if there was something nice she could do for Vanessa.

A few minutes later Martina stood at the edge of the rink and waited for her cue from the assistant director.

"Places!" he called out.

Martina took her place in the center of the ice just as Jake called out, "We're rolling!"

The music began, and Martina began to circle the rink. Once she began skating, she felt completely at ease. She flew along the surface of the ice, feeling more and more like Luci Ramirez. She loved the way the costume moved with her and the way it felt to be under the spotlight.

This must be what it's like to be a professional, Martina thought. She pretended she was skating in the Ice Capades.

She focused so intently on her skating that she forgot about everything else. When the music finished, she was stunned to hear wild applause.

Jake stood and shouted, "That's a take!" Even the crew went wild.

"Nice going!" one camera operator called out. "Perfect on the first try!"

Jake put an arm around Martina's shoulders. "Fabulous!" he said. "Really fabulous!"

Martina felt ecstatic as she skated off the ice. Everyone was congratulating her. The crew members all said how rare it was to perform perfectly on the first take. The cast kept telling her what a fantastic skater she was.

Vanessa flashed her a huge smile. "Smashing!" she said.

The whirlwind of praise died down seconds later, and Vanessa was called to the set.

Back to business, Martina thought. She'd had her few minutes in the spotlight, and now it was Vanessa's turn.

Martina positioned herself on the all-too-familiar bench to watch Vanessa's big dramatic scene.

Martina was anxious to see Vanessa perform this particular scene. It dramatized the famous event that had taken place right before Luci skated her *Pirates* routine in the Olympics. Martina had heard the story from Kathy, whose coach had been at the Olympics.

It had all started after Lydia Turnokova skated her long program. She'd been coming off the ice to get her scores. Luci, who was skating next, had been waiting to get on the ice. Lydia had walked past Luci and made a nasty remark, loud enough for Luci to hear, to the effect that Luci would probably get a high score from the Spanish-speaking judge.

According to Kathy's coach, a huge shouting match between Luci and Lydia had broken out right there beside the rink. The two skaters had come very close to fighting. Security guards had pulled them apart seconds before any punches were thrown. The story had made newspaper headlines around the world.

Vanessa and Jordana Moore—the actress who was playing Lydia Turnokova in the movie—took their places on the set.

Jake called, "Action!" and the two actresses began the scene.

Martina watched excitedly. She hadn't even been born when these Olympic games took place, but this was the next-best thing to being there.

Vanessa spoke her first line. "You were great out there tonight, Lydia."

Jordana's reply was jeering. "I know. If you're lucky, maybe you'll take home the silver medal."

Vanessa stepped forward. "Don't count me out of the race for the gold so fast," she replied. "I'm feeling pretty confident tonight."

Jordana made a face. "Confident that one of the judges is on your side?" she asked slyly.

"What's that supposed to mean?" Vanessa demanded.

"Oh, please! It's obvious who the *Hispanic* judge will give the highest score to."

Vanessa took a step closer to Jordana. "Are you implying that if I win a medal, it will be only because I'm Hispanic?"

"Cut!" Jake shouted suddenly. "You're just *saying* the lines, Vanessa. I want to see you *acting* them! Let's do it again. From the beginning."

Vanessa and Jordana began the scene again, and Jake stopped them in the same exact place. "Again!" he ordered.

Minutes turned into hours, and before long Martina was yawning and picking at her cuticles. Then she counted the lights on the ceiling, and after that, the bleachers. All this sitting around! It was making her nuts.

Meanwhile, on the set, Vanessa was having major problems, desperately trying to get through the scene. Jake had called "Cut!" so many times, it was embarrassing. He kept yelling at Vanessa for "more emotion," but Vanessa just wasn't catching on.

Martina couldn't understand why Vanessa was having so much trouble. It was obvious to *her* how Luci had felt back then.

By late afternoon, Jake was beside himself. So were the cast and crew. Everyone was frustrated and impatient.

"Take it from the top, *again!*" Jake grumbled.

Vanessa sighed loudly. "I'm sorry," she said irritably. "Where was I supposed to stand again?"

The lighting director groaned, and Jake buried his face in his hands. He called for a one-hour break. Vanessa walked off the set and out to her trailer without a word to anyone.

Martina was thrilled to get off "her bench," as she now thought of it. It was three o'clock, and her friends had promised to come by before Silver Blades practice. They were waiting in the lobby when Martina found them.

"Yogurt shake?" Amber asked, pointing to the snack bar.

"Make it two!" Martina groaned. "And an ice pack to sit on—I think I've lost all feeling in my rear end!"

In the snack bar, the girls found a table and ordered their shakes.

"What's up?" Nikki asked as they sipped. "You seem frazzled."

"Oh, it's murder in there!" Martina replied, motioning toward the rink. "It's Vanessa! She's *awful!*"

Haley laughed. "Really? How?"

"It's this one scene," Martina explained. "It's where Luci and Lydia have their big fight at the Olympics. Luci is supposed to be really angry, but Vanessa makes it seem as if she's only slightly upset." Martina took a sip of her shake and sat back. "I tell you, I've heard that scene so many times already, I can do it myself!"

Nikki's eyes lit up, and she, Haley, and Amber exchanged glances.

"Do it!" Nikki cried. "Come on, Tee! Do it!"

Martina slumped in her seat and giggled. "Yeah, *right!*"

"Oh, come on, Martina!" Haley urged. "Please? It'll be so funny!"

"Yeah, come on! Do it for us!" Amber begged.

Martina rolled her eyes, then looked at her friends. Why not? It *would* be fun. And she needed a good laugh.

She stood up from her seat and gazed around to make sure no one was watching. Then she got into character.

"You were great out there tonight, Lydia," Martina said. She waited a few seconds for Lydia's imaginary lines.

"Don't count me out of the race for the gold so fast, Lydia!" Martina went on. "I'm feeling pretty confident tonight."

Martina waited a few more seconds. Then she gasped. "What's that supposed to mean?" she asked angrily. She put her hands on her hips and stared at the air next to her, where she pretended Lydia Turnokova was standing. She took a step toward the invisible Lydia.

Martina felt the anger boiling inside her. She knew exactly how Luci must have felt after Lydia's insult.

"Are you implying," she said in an angry voice, "that if I win a medal, it will be only because I'm Hispanic?"

Martina waited a few seconds, then turned back into Martina again. She gave a silly, dramatic bow, and her friends all stood up and cheered.

Martina was still bent over in her bow when she heard a familiar voice behind her. "Nice work."

Martina straightened up and whirled around. She nearly choked. It was Jake Collins!

11

Martina felt her face turn bright red. She tried desperately to smile. How much had Jake seen? she wondered.

"Uh, hi," she finally managed to say. She bit her bottom lip and pointed to the booth where her friends sat. "We were just, uh, eating lunch, and, uh, goofing around, you know. . . ." She knew she wasn't speaking in coherent sentences, but what else could she do? She'd been caught, and she felt totally humiliated.

Jake, though, didn't seem the least bit interested. The director was already walking away, deep in conversation with a man beside him.

When Jake was out of sight, Martina fell into the booth and laid her head down on the table. "I, Martina Nemo, am the world's biggest jerk!" she moaned.

"Wasn't that the director?" Haley asked.

Martina raised her head. "Yes, that was the director!

And I made such a fool of myself in front of him! He must think I'm a spoiled brat to make fun of Vanessa like that." She shook her head, miserable. "I should never have done it. It was mean."

"He didn't seem to care," Nikki pointed out. "Oh, don't worry, Tee. He's probably forgotten about it already."

Martina stared at her yogurt shake but couldn't drink it. Her stomach was too shaky. She played with the straw while her friends gossiped about Silver Blades. Martina only half listened. She was too busy worrying about Jake Collins and what he'd seen her do.

Soon it was time to go back to rehearsal. Martina said good-bye to her friends and returned to the rink. She took her place on her bench and waited for the shooting to start. Meanwhile, she watched Vanessa goofing around with one of the camera guys, pretending to turn the camera on him. They were both laughing, having a great time.

Martina wondered why Vanessa was playing around. She should have been practicing the scene that was giving her so much trouble.

Oh, well. It's not my problem, Martina decided.

Jake Collins took his place in the director's chair. They were ready to begin again. Martina watched him say a few words quietly to Vanessa. Vanessa grimaced. She walked briskly back to the set, stood in her starting place next to Jordana Moore, and folded her arms across her chest.

A stagehand walked in front of Vanessa and held a

clapboard in front of her face. He snapped it loudly, then called out, "Scene twenty. Take twenty-three."

Has it really been twenty-three takes? Martina wondered. Yikes!

When Jake called, "Action!" all eyes were on Vanessa. Martina crossed her fingers and held her breath, praying Vanessa would get it right this time. She really didn't feel like sitting on the bench for the rest of the day.

Vanessa closed her eyes. Martina hoped she was becoming one with her character.

Then Vanessa said her first line. "You were great out there tonight, Jordana."

Everyone laughed until Jake shouted for quiet.

The rink fell silent.

"What?" Vanessa asked.

Martina groaned. Vanessa was still clueless.

Jake got up from his chair. "You said 'Jordana,' " he told the actress in quiet, cutting tones. The line is 'You were great out there tonight, *Lydia.*' "

Vanessa stared at the ground. "Sorry," she mumbled.

"Do it again!" Jake ordered.

Vanessa started the scene again, but Jake stopped her after her third line. "No! No!" he shouted at Vanessa. "How many times do I have to tell you? You're supposed to get angry here!"

Jake began to pace back and forth furiously. "Vanessa, what is with you today?" he demanded. "You're completely off. You're making stupid mistakes, and you're not listening to me. Do you think this is all a big game?"

Vanessa's eyes widened. "Oh, no, Jake. I—"

Jake interrupted her. "No excuses. You had plenty of time to rehearse this scene. You're not getting it at all! If you don't try harder, I swear I'll get someone else—"

Suddenly Jake stopped talking. He scanned the bleachers until his eyes found Martina.

"Martina!" he called out. "Take the set, please."

Martina gulped. "Me?" she asked, getting up from the bench.

"Yes," Jake said. "Come on. Hurry. Take the set next to Jordana."

Martina swallowed nervously. She walked onto the set and stood next to Jordana.

"Martina," Jake said calmly, "would you please show Vanessa how the scene is supposed to be done?"

"*Huh?*" Martina nearly choked. Was he serious?

"Just like you did it this afternoon in the snack bar," Jake said.

Martina didn't dare look at Vanessa's face, but she could feel the actress staring at her.

"I—I . . . don't think I can," Martina stammered.

"Martina, please! We're already way behind schedule. Please! Just do the scene with Jordana. The same way I saw you do it earlier."

"But—"

Jake strode onto the set and stood in front of Martina. "Listen," he said. "You're Luci Ramirez. You're about to skate the most important routine of your life. Then you bump into Lydia—your fiercest competition. She insults you. Insults your skating ability. And your heritage. What do you do? Come on, Martina! Say the lines!"

Listening to Jake, Martina got caught up in the scene again. She cleared her throat and tried to remember all the acting advice her father had given her. Naturally, her mind went completely blank. All that went through her head was her father saying over and over again, "Become one with your character. Become one with your character."

And Martina became Luci. She turned to Jordana. "What is that supposed to mean?" she demanded.

"Good! Good, Martina! Keep going!" Jake whispered.

"Are you implying that if I win a medal, it will be only because I'm Hispanic?"

As Martina spoke the lines she felt strange, as if she were listening to someone else speak. She was so into what she was feeling and what she was saying, she almost forgot where she was.

When she finished, she took a deep breath. She turned to see Jake smiling at her.

"Martina, that was fabulous," he said.

Martina broke into a huge grin at Jake's compliment. But her smile froze when she saw Vanessa. Vanessa was glaring at Martina with complete and total fury.

Martina immediately tried to explain. "Vanessa, I didn't mean—"

"Okay, Martina, thank you," Jake Collins called out, interrupting her. "You can take your seat again."

"But—"

"Thank you, Martina," he repeated more firmly.

Martina gulped and returned to her bench. Her

hands were shaking. She felt about as big as a flea. How could she have done that to Vanessa? Especially after Vanessa had been so nice to her.

Martina felt rotten. She sat nervously on the bench for the rest of the day. After rehearsal, she rushed over to Vanessa and tried to explain.

"Vanessa, I didn't mean for that to happen," Martina began. But Vanessa turned her back on Martina and headed for her trailer.

"Vanessa! Please listen to me!" Martina called after her. She knew the actress heard her. But Vanessa didn't stop or turn around. "I only did it because Jake asked me to, and I thought—"

Martina stopped talking. What was the use? Vanessa didn't care a thing about her explanation. The bottom line was that she'd embarrassed Vanessa—in front of everyone. She'd humiliated an experienced actress on the set of her own movie.

Great, Martina thought with dismay. Now the star of the movie hates me. Way to go, Martina.

"**P**ass the General Tso's chicken," Martina said to her brother across the dinner table.

Richard lifted the carton of Chinese food. He was handing it to Martina when Mr. Nemo grabbed it from his hands.

"Ask for the chicken with more *emotion*, Martina," her father said. "Pretend you've been stranded on a desert island for years. You've been dreaming of General Tso's chicken all that time. Now you gaze longingly at the chicken and lick your lips. Beads of perspiration drip down—"

"Dad!" Martina cried. "Just pass the chicken, okay?"

"Can I help it if I'm excited?" Mr. Nemo asked. "My daughter just acted her heart out in front of a real Hollywood director!"

Martina stood and grabbed the carton of chicken from her father, then bowed to the rest of her family.

"That was Martina Nemo, the actress, working on yet another emotion. *Hunger!*"

The rest of her family cracked up—even the baby smiled.

"You can laugh all you want, sweetie, but I heard you were terrific today!" Mr. Nemo was beaming.

"Don't you mean *smashing* or *fabulous*?" Martina joked.

Her father seemed confused.

"Those are Hollywood words," Martina explained. "That's what everyone says all day. 'You were absolutely smashing! That dress is fabulous!' "

Richard made a face. "Really? Yuck."

Martina nodded. "I know what you mean."

"Well, when you become a famous actress," Mr. Nemo said, "you can make up some Hollywood words of your own."

"Dad," Martina said patiently, "I don't want to be an actress. I want to be a skater."

"Why not do both?" Martina's mother suggested.

"Well, if I can skate with the Ice Capades," Martina said, "then I *will* do both."

Mr. Nemo didn't look content with that. "I think after this movie is finished and you have the experience, you can audition for another movie. I know a talent agent from when I was acting in New York, and—"

"Wait! Just wait, Dad!" Martina interrupted. "I just *said* I don't want to be an actress. I want to *skate*!"

"When you're a movie star, will you get us into your movies for free?" Richard asked.

Martina groaned. Hadn't anybody heard a word she'd said?

"Will you have a dressing room?" Gabriella asked.

Martina shook her head. Nobody was listening to her. "Okay," she said. "For the gazillionth time, I don't want to be an actress. I just want to be a professional skater. With the Ice Capades!"

Everyone stared at her.

"Do they give you a dressing room in the Ice Capades?" Richard asked. "Or do you get a trailer?"

Hearing the mention of a trailer reminded Martina of Vanessa and what had happened earlier. She thought about Vanessa's face that afternoon, how the actress had stared at her in total shock. I wonder what she thinks of me, Martina thought. She must hate me. She must think I'm out to steal her part!

The phone rang. Gabriella jumped to get it.

"It's Nikki!" she told Martina.

Martina grabbed a fork and the carton of General Tso's chicken and bounced up from the table. "I'm gonna take it upstairs, okay?"

Her parents nodded.

Martina raced upstairs. "I got it!" she cried down to Gabriella. After her sister hung up the extension, Martina blurted out, "Guess what?"

"What?" Nikki asked.

"Remember that little scene I did at the snack bar today?"

"Uh-huh."

"Well, the director asked me to do it again," Martina said. "On the set, in front of everyone!"

Nikki shrieked so loudly, Martina had to pull the phone away from her ear. "Get out of here!" Nikki cried. "Tell me everything!"

Martina explained everything that had happened, without leaving out a single detail. She told Nikki how Vanessa had stormed away after rehearsal, refusing to listen to her explanation.

"I always knew there was something sneaky about that girl!" Nikki said.

"What are you talking about?" Martina asked. "She's been very nice."

"Remember Elyse Taylor?" Nikki asked.

"Oh, Vanessa's not that bad!" Martina said defensively. Martina had heard stories about Elyse Taylor, the skating star. Elyse had visited Silver Blades a while ago. Everyone had been excited to meet her, until they found out how mean and nasty she could be. They'd ended up calling her the Ice Princess.

"I don't know," Nikki said. "I just get that same feeling about Vanessa, you know? Anyway, don't worry about her. She'll get over it. It's probably not the first time it's happened. Remember when we read about her jealous rages on the set of *Hollywood High*?"

Martina did remember reading that. Still, Vanessa had been nice to her.

"And anyway," Nikki went on, "the director thinks you're a good actress! Maybe he can help you skate in another movie after this."

"Maybe," Martina replied. "I'd better get going. I have to be at the rink at four A.M. again tomorrow to meet with Blake."

"Okay, Tee. See you tomorrow."

After helping clear the dinner table, Martina showered and got ready for bed. It was only eight, but she was exhausted. Still a week to go—then maybe she'd get some rest. Although she was sure she'd have mounds of schoolwork piled up, even after her tutoring began on the set.

Martina fell into bed and rubbed her tired eyes. She stared at the ceiling for a minute or so and thought about the Ice Capades. It was all she thought about these days. She loved skating and the theater, so naturally a combination of the two would be perfect.

She closed her eyes and thought about the events of that day. She really wished things had gone differently with Vanessa. Despite what Nikki had said about Vanessa, Martina still liked her. She figured she'd try talking to Vanessa again the next morning.

Martina was drifting off to sleep when she suddenly found herself in the middle of an enormous ice rink. She was waving to her cheering fans in the stands. Flowers of every kind were dropping at her feet.

Out of nowhere, the music from *Pirates of Penzance* came on, and Martina glanced down. She was wearing a pirate's costume! She lunged forward and instinctively began skating Luci's routine. Applause surrounded her. Suddenly she felt the presence of someone else on the ice. She dug her blades into the ice and came to a stop.

Vanessa Guzman was coming toward her on skates.

"Hi, Vanessa!" Martina said with a wave.

Vanessa didn't answer. She scowled at Martina and

skated closer. Martina noticed Vanessa was dressed like a pirate, too. And she was carrying a long, sharp sword.

Something didn't feel right. Martina began skating in the opposite direction. Vanessa began to pick up speed. Soon the two girls were racing across the ice, which somehow had turned into a skating rink on a pirate ship. Martina glanced over her shoulder and saw Pirate Vanessa draw her sword.

Martina's body shook with fear. "But Vanessa," she cried over her shoulder, "I didn't mean it! Really!"

Vanessa threw her head back with an evil laugh. She skated faster and faster. Martina flew across the ice, trying to escape the evil pirate.

Martina was going too fast to stop, and she skidded right over the side of the ship. Another few feet and she'd be shark food! She fell down . . . down . . . down . . .

Martina awoke with a start.

She sat up in bed and gazed around her room in confusion. It had been a dream. She wiped her forehead and took a deep breath.

First thing tomorrow, she promised herself, I'll find Vanessa and try to explain.

13

Martina sat on the ice and stared at Blake, waiting for his comments.

"Nice, Martina!" Blake called to her. "Let's do it again."

Martina stood up and wiped the ice shavings off her warm-up leggings. She was incredibly sore. She'd been falling all morning. My thighs must be black and blue by now, she thought tiredly.

"Terrific fall, Martina," Blake told her. "You went down perfectly."

Martina let out a tired laugh. It was a strange thing to hear that she had messed up perfectly. But that was what this particular scene in the movie called for. Martina was learning Luci Ramirez's short program from her debut at the Regionals. The routine was simple, really, but it called for her to mess up on a spiral step sequence—exactly as Luci had.

Martina stretched, then glanced across the ice for the hundredth time. Across the rink, Andie was blocking a scene with Jake. Martina searched for Vanessa but didn't see her anywhere.

"Think you'll be ready to shoot this scene this afternoon?" Blake asked her.

Martina thought for a second, then nodded. "Sure. But I'd like to keep practicing—just to be as confident as possible." She rubbed her rear again, wondering how many more bumps on the ice her body could take.

Blake had her practice the scene for most of the day. Afterward Martina was sent to Kirsten for her next costume fitting. She smiled when she saw the outfit. It wasn't as elaborate as the *Pirates* costume had been, but it would definitely be fun to wear.

It was a simple skating dress. What made it really cool was that the right side was black and the left side was white. Half and half exactly. Martina thought it was kind of funky.

Once in costume, Martina was ready for Gustav. Before getting settled in the makeup chair, she checked the information board to see what time she was wanted on the set. The newly posted schedule said three o'clock.

Martina sat in the makeup chair while Gustav worked on her face. He put that cakey gook on her face again, then outlined her eyes with black eyeliner. With the costume, it was a very dramatic look.

A little before three, Martina took a seat on "her bench." She was happy to see Andie was still with the director. She hoped she'd get a chance to hang out with Andie a bit before her call. But at three exactly, the assistant director called her name.

Martina got up from the bench. Something nagged at her—it felt as though her laces were loose. That's weird, she thought. I just tightened them.

There wasn't much light in the rink, so she couldn't inspect her skates more closely. And she didn't want to keep Jake waiting. So she tied them as tightly as possible, then skated onto the ice and got into position for the scene.

As she waited for Jake to call "Action!" Martina took another look around the arena for Vanessa. She didn't see her anywhere. She *did* see a familiar face over by the director's chair, though. When she realized who it was, her mouth fell open.

Tori!

Martina couldn't believe it. What's Tori doing here again? she wondered. Mrs. Carsen was sitting at her daughter's right, and on Mrs. Carsen's right was Kirsten. The three looked like old friends, laughing about something. Tori was wearing another new skating costume—one Martina had never seen before.

Martina's stomach churned. What was going on? She stared hard at Tori, hoping to catch her eye. Tori avoided Martina's gaze completely.

This is too much, Martina thought. Now Tori is buddy-buddy with Kirsten. Martina had to find out why Tori was there. It didn't make sense. When she learned she hadn't gotten a part in the movie, Tori had turned up her nose at the whole idea of filming the movie in Seneca Hills, but here she was, all chummy with the crew!

Martina felt a twinge of jealousy. After all, this was *her* movie. Tori had nothing to do with it!

When Jake called, "Lights! Camera!" Martina struck her starting pose. Forget about Tori, she told herself. Just concentrate on skating! Then the music started, and Martina pushed off into her routine.

The first thirty seconds of her program went smoothly, Martina's soreness disappeared as she lost herself in the quick, light rhythm of the routine. But suddenly her left foot came out from under her and she fell.

Martina sat on the ice for a second, stunned. How could she have messed up such an easy jump? She did them all the time. In fact, she hadn't messed up this particular move in months. Then she spied her left skate. Sure enough, the lace had come undone.

"Cut!" Jake cried. "Take it from the top again, Martina!"

"I'm sorry!" she called back to him. "But my skate is—"

"Just do it again!" Jake shouted. "We're way behind today, so hurry! Take two!"

Martina bent down to pull her laces tighter. A sense of dread went through her as one of the laces snapped off right in her hand. Oh, no! she thought nervously.

The music suddenly began again. All Martina could do was stand frozen on the ice, holding the broken lace.

She felt stupid just standing there, but what else could she do? It was too dangerous to skate with a broken lace. She felt tears form in her eyes.

Finally Martina spotted Blake and skated quickly in his direction. She showed him the broken lace, and he immediately went over to Jake. Martina saw the impatient look on the director's face as Blake explained what had happened. Blake returned with Kirsten, and Kirsten inspected Martina's skates.

"Did you cut the laces?" Kirsten asked as she replaced the laces with a fresh pair.

Martina's eyes widened. "No! Why?"

"These were definitely cut," Kirsten said, showing Martina part of the broken lace. "Someone cut them partway. When you skated, they broke completely."

"You mean somebody cut my laces?" Martina asked in shock. "Deliberately?"

Kirsten shrugged. "Well, I can't be one hundred percent sure, but it looks that way. Of course, it could have been an accident. That skater over there, do you know her?" She gestured at Tori.

Martina looked in that direction, too. Tori glanced away almost immediately.

"Yeah, why?" Martina asked in confusion.

Kirsten continued relacing the other skate. "Well, she was in the room with your skates earlier."

Martina was dumbfounded. "Earlier?" she asked.

Kirsten nodded. "Her mother came by to say hello while I was touching up your costume. Tori was looking at the skates. I wondered about it, but I figured she just had a flair for fashion," she added. "Like her mother. Corinne Carsen and I went to the same fashion-design school in New York City, you know."

Martina sat listening as Kirsten went on about fashion school. The thoughts that were running through her head frightened her. *Tori was in the dressing room today. Tori was handling these skates. And then I almost broke my neck out there . . .*

Could Tori be that jealous of me? Martina wondered. *Did she cut my laces—just so I'd fall and mess up?*

Martina swallowed hard. *Tori Carsen is trying to get me kicked off this movie!*

14

Martina took to the ice again with new laces on her skates. She was nervous and shaky. She could sense Tori's eyes on her, waiting for her to mess up again.

Well, Tori, Martina muttered under her breath, I'm not going to give you the satisfaction!

Martina stopped trembling as she began the routine. She hit every move and finished the sequence smoothly. She struck her final pose confidently. She even held it for a few seconds longer than she had to. Jake called, "Cut!" Martina heard him groan.

"Martina! You forgot to fall!" Blake called.

Martina stared at him in confusion. She'd been so busy trying to show Tori what a great skater she was, she'd forgotten to mess up the spiral step sequence!

"I'm sorry, Blake," she apologized. "I won't forget next time."

"Good." Blake went back to talk to the director. Soon

the set was ready for take three. At that moment Martina finally spotted Vanessa. The actress was standing next to Jake with a smug smile across her face.

Vanessa sure seems glad that she's not the one messing up this time! Martina thought.

Martina took her starting position for the third time. She made it through the entire short program—fall and all. As she stood in her final pose she waited to hear clapping. This time there wasn't any. Martina skated off the ice and back to the bench. Blake appeared moments later.

"Great job," he told her.

Martina shrugged. Blake was probably just trying to be nice.

"Come on," he said. "We still have a lot to do today. Jake wants to shoot the scene where Luci comes off the ice after her silver-medal win at the Worlds."

"But I don't know that program!" Martina said in alarm.

"Don't worry," Blake said calmly. "The whole program isn't part of the film. Just the last three moves."

Martina followed him to the opposite end of the rink. Blake began to teach her the moves.

Just as Martina landed a lovely waltz jump she glanced up and spotted Tori across the ice. Tori had changed into a gorgeous new costume that was bright pink with white fur trim. And she was skating in front of Jake Collins!

Martina lost her position. She put her hands on her hips. "Why is Tori skating?" she asked.

Blake gazed across the ice and shrugged. "Don't

know," he replied. "But get your mind back on the routine. We have to have it ready in a few hours."

Martina practiced the moves until she felt confident. They were pretty simple moves, really, and she was sure she'd be fine in front of the cameras. When she had them down she headed for the costume department and found the elegant red skating dress she was supposed to wear for the scene. She put it on and went to find Gustav.

As she sat in the makeup chair, Martina heard an announcement about the new shooting schedule being posted on the information board. As soon as Gustav finished with her, she stopped in the lobby to see what time she was wanted on the set. A small card was pinned to the board. It read, NEMO—8:00 P.M.

Martina glanced up at the clock to check the time. It was a little after six. There was plenty of time for her to grab a quick bite, then head over to the ballet room to stretch out and work on her form.

At the snack bar, Martina ended up ordering just a cola. She didn't want to ruin Gustav's makeup job by chewing. It was pretty empty in the Arena, since Silver Blades and Hawks practice had ended at five-thirty. With no one to talk to, she finished her drink and walked over to the ballet room.

Martina was examining her layback position in the mirror when Blake came bursting through the door in a panic.

"Martina!" he cried frantically. "What's going on? You were supposed to be on the set half an hour ago!"

Martina looked at the clock above the door. "But it's only seven-thirty!" she protested. "The note said eight!"

Blake shook his head. "No, Martina, it said seven! Come on! They're holding everything up, waiting for you!"

Martina's stomach began to churn as she grabbed her skates and followed Blake to the rink. How could this have happened? She was positive the note had said eight.

At the rink, Jake Collins was pacing frantically. He took one look at Martina and lost it.

"Do you know how far behind schedule we are?" he bellowed. Martina saw a vein throb near his temple. "This is going to cost us thousands of dollars in production costs! For every second you're late, I'm paying for technicians, equipment—"

"I—I'm s-so sorry," Martina began apologizing. She felt a knot in her stomach the size of a snowball, and tears formed in the corners of her eyes. "I thought I was supposed—"

"Never mind!" Jake cut her off. "Just get on the set. And from now on," he warned, "if you can't make it here on time, we'll find another skater who can!"

Martina sat slumped on the sofa in the den with the TV remote control in her hand. Mindlessly she flipped through the channels, stopping briefly on a rerun of *Hollywood High.*

Vanessa was on-screen, playing the role of Mackenzie Phipps. Mackenzie was threatening a girl in the school bathroom. "If you tell Joelle it was me, I'll ruin you," she warned. "I didn't go to all this trouble to fail science!"

Martina watched Vanessa act the scene and chuckled softly. Mackenzie Phipps was so rich and so obnoxious on the show—maybe that was why Nikki had all those bad feelings about Vanessa. Meanwhile, Martina hadn't even had a chance to talk to Vanessa yet. And every day she didn't, she felt worse and worse.

Martina sighed loudly, then changed the channel. It had been a really crummy day. On a scale of one to ten, a definite one. And she'd only given it that one point because she had managed to complete a scene successfully. The rest of the day's events, however, she wished she could do all over again.

The phone rang in the Nemo house, and Martina reached over to answer it.

"You're home!" Nikki said cheerfully. "So how'd it go today? Are you packing for Hollywood yet?"

"Not exactly."

Nikki noticed the tone in Martina's voice right away. "What's the matter, Tee?" she asked. "When I peeked in at you this afternoon, I thought you looked great. What happened?"

Martina told Nikki about the completely horrible day she'd had, from the broken lace right up to Jake's threat.

"Oooh, you must have wanted to die," Nikki sympathized.

"You should have seen his face!" Martina said. "He was furious!"

"But the note said eight. How could it have been wrong?"

"I know! How could it have been? Blake wouldn't make a mistake like that. And I know what I saw. I wish I knew what *really* happened," Martina muttered.

"What are you saying, Tee?" Nikki asked.

Martina wasn't sure how to answer. On the one hand, Nikki was her best friend. She should be able to tell her anything. The problem was, Nikki was also a good friend of Tori's. And Nikki and Tori had been friends for much longer. Martina wondered if she could tell Nikki that she thought Tori was the one doing all these horrible things.

"Okay, here's the thing," Martina said slowly. "I have a weird feeling about all this."

"What do you mean?"

"First, the laces. Kirsten said they might have been cut deliberately. And T—" She stopped herself from saying Tori's name. "—*someone* was really interested in those particular skates."

"Really?"

"Yes. And the note. I'm *positive* it said eight o'clock, but Blake insists it said seven. He says he wrote it, so he should know. So I'm thinking, someone could have changed it."

"The same person who cut the laces?" Nikki asked.

"Yes," Martina replied.

"So who do you think it is?" Nikki asked.

Martina bit her bottom lip. "Okay, now, I'm not trying to be mean or anything, and it's *possible* I could be wrong, but . . ."

"Tell me!" Nikki urged.

"Tori," Martina said bluntly.

"Tori?"

"It makes sense, Nikki," Martina said. "Tori was in the room with my skates! Then I saw her hanging around late today—way after Silver Blades practice. She could have easily changed the note on the board."

"Are you sure, Tee?"

"Well," Martina went on, "Tori's been acting so weird around me lately—nasty, too. She and her mother are at all the shootings, even though the director closed the set. And today," Martina added, "she was wearing a brand-new skating costume and skating for the director!"

Nikki was quiet for a moment. "Yeah, I asked Tori about that yesterday. She acted all mysterious and everything and didn't answer me. It's possible that her mother put her up to something." Nikki hesitated a moment. "Tee, Tori may be jealous and stuck up at times, but I think I know her pretty well. She would never do anything to harm a friend. She knows how dangerous it would be for you to skate with cut laces."

Martina thought about that for a moment. Nikki was right. Tori would know better. Still . . .

"Well, I don't know," Martina mumbled. "Something weird is definitely going on."

"I'll talk to Tori for you tomorrow if you want," Nikki offered. "But really, Tee, I don't think Tori would do those things to you. She likes you."

Martina didn't answer. If Tori liked her so much, then why had she been acting so mean lately, saying all those obnoxious things and avoiding Martina like the plague? Plus, if Tori was supposed to be her friend, then why couldn't she be happy for Martina—the way all her other friends were?

"Okay, whatever," Martina said. "But I should go. It's getting late. By the way, how's school? Am I missing much?"

Nikki laughed. "Oh, right. I almost forgot. Check out what happened in the lunchroom today. . . ."

Martina listened to Nikki talk about what sounded like the craziest food fight Grandview Middle School had ever seen. She actually wished she could have been there. She sighed, thinking about all the catching up she'd have to do once the movie was finished. Not only catching up on her schoolwork, but on her social life as well.

Martina hung up the phone and turned off the TV. She headed for the stairs to her bedroom. She stopped when she saw her father, Richard, and Gabriella rehearsing *Grease* in the living room. Her father had his hair slicked back and was wearing goofy 1950s clothes. Gabriella was holding a pad and a pen in her hand.

"What can I get for you?" Gabriella said slowly. A smile broke out across her face. "Did you hear, Martina? That's my line. Daddy said I could be in the play, too!"

Mr. Nemo smiled. "It's true," he said. "I felt that two famous Nemos just weren't enough, so I managed to get a small role for Gaby in *Grease*."

"Wow! That's great, Gaby!" Martina exclaimed. She wished she had her sister's guts when it came to performing. Gabriella never had stage fright.

"What can I get for you?" Gabriella said again.

"See how good she is?" Mr. Nemo asked. "It's in the blood, I tell you!"

Martina frowned. "Dad, I'm sorry to break it to you, but after today, I think my acting career might just be over," she said sadly.

Mr. Nemo took his daughter's hand. "Listen, sweetheart. In the theater there are good days and bad days. You just had a bad day. Forget it and move on."

Martina thought about it for a moment and realized her father was right. She'd just had a bad day. It was time to forget all about it and move on.

Tomorrow will be a *good* day, Martina told herself as she climbed the stairs.

15

Martina made it to the rink at four the next morning. It was earlier than she needed to be there, but she wanted to give her muscles a workout before Blake came in. That day he was supposed to show her Luci's world-famous exhibition routine from the European Figure-Skating Championships. Martina could hardly wait. It was one of the first times that Luci had performed her famous unassisted death spiral. The spectacular spin had been known as the Ramirez spiral ever since.

Blake was surprised to see Martina already skating when he got there. "Good morning!" he said.

Martina looked up from her footwork sequence. Blake was smiling. She had a feeling she'd been forgiven for messing up the day before.

"I want you to know, Martina," he said seriously, "I think you're doing a great job. And I managed to calm

Jake down yesterday, so don't worry. Just promise me one thing. Promise you'll be extra careful around him from now on. Be on time—even early, if you can."

Martina nodded. "I promise."

"Yesterday was a pretty rough day for all of us," Blake went on. "Jake has a lot to worry about with this movie—production costs, schedules, and all sorts of other stuff. So don't let what he said yesterday get to you."

Martina felt a little better.

Blake clasped his hands together. "Okay. Enough about that. Are you ready to learn the Ramirez spiral?"

Martina grinned. "Definitely!" she replied. "But Blake, what if I can't do it perfectly?"

"Don't worry," Blake said. "Just do your best. And remember, we'll work a little movie magic on it. The spiral's a tough move, Martina. No one expects you to do it perfectly. At least not by five o'clock today."

Martina's eyes widened. "Five o'clock? But I—"

"I said don't worry. You'll do fine. We have a full dress rehearsal at five tonight, and Jake's hoping to film the scene early tomorrow morning. He can add in some special effects later, to make it look as though you really did an unassisted death spiral."

"Okay," Martina replied. She didn't understand how anyone could make her look as though she were doing a perfect Ramirez spiral. She'd have to do a halfway decent one for them to work with.

By twelve-thirty Martina was tired and hungry. Blake insisted she take a lunch break. The problem was, there wasn't anybody around for her to eat with. Silver Blades practice wouldn't start for another three hours.

Martina made her way over to the snack bar. Her stomach was rumbling—she couldn't wait to order a turkey sandwich.

Martina gave her order to the woman at the sandwich counter. Then she searched for a table. When she turned around, she saw Vanessa Guzman.

Finally! Martina thought. She'd been trying to talk to Vanessa for days now with no luck. Now was her chance to apologize for the other day. She made her way over to where the actress was sitting alone, reading a book.

Martina approached Vanessa's table slowly, waiting for her to look up. When she finally did, Vanessa scowled.

"Vanessa, do you have a sec?" Martina asked.

Vanessa made a big deal about checking her watch, then sighed. "I guess I have a minute," she replied distractedly.

Martina took a deep breath. "It's about the other day. I didn't mean for any of that to happen! Jake forced me to do the scene, and I—"

Vanessa held up a hand and stopped her. "Look. Forget about it, will you? It's no big deal. It's not like I'm worried you'll steal my part or anything. And I don't really feel like talking about it anymore, okay?" She snapped her book shut and stood up. "I don't blame you, Miranda," she went on, "but I'd like to get past this. Got it?"

Martina stood frozen in place, hurt by the actress's cold tone. Clearly Vanessa was still furious. And had she really forgotten Martina's name?

"Uh, yeah, sure," Martina mumbled awkwardly. "I—"

"Fine!" Vanessa snapped, flinging her handbag over her shoulder. She turned and walked away, leaving a half-eaten salad and a cola.

"And it's Martina, not Miranda!" Martina called after her. Vanessa didn't hear her. She was already out the door.

So much for making amends.

"Turkey sandwich!" the woman at the counter called out.

Martina took her food and sat down by herself. She'd been starving, but now her appetite was gone. What is Vanessa's problem, anyway? she wondered. Why couldn't she just accept my apology? She must know it wasn't totally my fault. After all, it was Jake's idea.

Martina ate her sandwich in silence, then spent the rest of her lunch break in the ballet room, working on her moves in front of the mirrors.

For the next two hours Martina and Blake practiced the Ramirez spiral. Martina arched her back until her head nearly touched the floor.

"You're doing great!" Blake assured her.

Martina wished she could actually do the Ramirez spiral on her own, without movie magic. Wouldn't that be something? Her friends in Silver Blades would certainly be impressed.

Soon it was time to be fitted and made up for the dress rehearsal. Martina hurried to the locker room to freshen up. She peeked inside and saw Kirsten fitting Vanessa for the European Championships costume. Martina shut the door quickly when she saw them. She didn't feel like being near Vanessa right then. She'd come back when Vanessa was finished with her fitting.

She waited in the lobby for a little while, then walked over to the other rink. Silver Blades practice was going on. She sat in the bleachers and watched the skaters. Across the ice, she spotted Tori and Amber working on their double axels. Nikki was off practicing with Alex Beekman, her skating partner. Haley was talking to Kathy Bart.

"Homesick?" Tori asked as she skated past Martina. Her tone was cool, but it was the first time she'd spoken to Martina in days without saying anything rude or obnoxious.

"Checking up on us common folks?" Tori went on, skating past her a second time.

So much for not being rude or obnoxious.

"I'm just resting, Tori," Martina said flatly. "Don't make something out of it."

Tori stopped skating. "What's that supposed to mean?" she snapped.

Martina was tired of walking on eggshells around Tori. So what if Tori was jealous and couldn't handle losing the movie role? That wasn't Martina's problem.

"For your information, Tori," Martina said, "I happen to like being in this movie. It's really important to me, so stop badmouthing it and giving me such a hard time. If you're too jealous to accept the fact that I got cast and you didn't, then just don't see the movie when it's shown on TV, okay?"

Martina knew *she* was the one being obnoxious now, but she didn't care. These things needed to be said. Especially because she was convinced that it was Tori who was trying to get her kicked off the movie.

Before Tori could wipe the shocked look from her face, Martina stormed away from the rink in disgust. She had more important things to do than square off with Tori. She had a movie to shoot.

Martina returned to the locker room. She was happy to see that Vanessa was gone.

"Here it is," Kirsten said, holding up the final costume. As soon as Martina laid eyes on it, she forgot about Tori and Vanessa and Jake and *everything*. She clasped her hands together excitedly. "Wow! Kirsten, it's awesome!"

Kirsten agreed. "It's my masterpiece," she said proudly. "I worked a long time on the design. It's a lot like Luci's, but I've changed it slightly and added my own special touches."

Martina gazed at the bright yellow satin and pictured herself wearing it, spinning in a Ramirez spiral on the ice beneath a bright spotlight. The costume was all yellow, except for the underskirt, which was bright orange. The skirt and the sleeves were ruffly and loose, and there were spangles and more ruffles across the front. It was absolutely gorgeous.

"I wish I could keep it after the movie," Martina sighed.

Kirsten laughed. "Don't hold your breath, my dear."

"Well, I'm just glad I get the chance to wear it!" Martina said.

At four-thirty Martina met Gustav for her makeup, then rushed back to pick up her costume. She didn't want to be even one second late for the dress rehearsal. She'd promised Blake—and herself—that for the rest of the movie she was going to be on Jake Collins's good side every single moment.

Kirsten wasn't around when Martina returned to the locker room, but the costume was hanging on a hook by the door. Seeing it again gave Martina the chills. It was *so* pretty! She couldn't wait to put it on.

She was about to get undressed when she suddenly realized she'd left her skates back at the rink. With a sigh, Martina pulled her red crewneck T-shirt back over her head, then neatly laid the costume on the bench next to her locker.

Martina rushed back to the rink to look for her skates. They were right where she'd left them—next to the makeup chair.

"Wait a minute," Gustav called as she picked up the skates. "You have a smudge on your left cheek. Come over here and let me fix it."

"Okay, but hurry," Martina pleaded with him. "I can't be late today!"

It seemed like forever before Gustav was done with her. Martina hurried back to the locker room, glancing at the clock. She still had ten minutes until her call—just enough time to get dressed and lace up her skates.

Martina opened the door to the locker room, pictur-

ing herself dressed in yellow satin. She went straight
to the bench next to her locker, where she'd laid out
the costume. It didn't take her long to notice that
something was very wrong.

The bench was empty. The bright yellow costume
was gone!

16

Where could the costume have gone?

Martina searched the locker room. The costume wasn't on the floor or on a bench. It wasn't in her locker. It wasn't anywhere! Taking a second to catch her breath, she went over the past ten minutes in her mind: She'd had the costume. She'd put the costume on the bench to go get her skates. She'd gotten her skates, had her makeup retouched, then returned to the locker room.

She was still no closer to finding the costume than before. Someone must have taken it, Martina realized. She swallowed hard. Tori!

Martina raced over to the costume-fitting area and looked for Kirsten or one of Kirsten's assistants. Nobody was there. She searched for the costume again, thinking—praying—that maybe Kirsten had seen it on the bench and hung it back on the hook. But it wasn't there either.

Martina began to panic. Her hands trembled, and she blinked back tears. She knew it must be five o'clock already. Jake Collins was *not* going to be happy.

Her next thought was to find Blake. Maybe he'd know what to do. She raced back to the rink and found the choreographer talking with a camera operator.

"Blake!" she whispered loudly.

He turned around and saw immediately that something was wrong. "Martina, what is it?" he asked.

Martina motioned for Blake to follow her into the lobby. Her voice shook as she explained the situation.

Blake's face paled. "Are you sure you looked everywhere?" he asked.

Martina nodded. "Well, just in the locker room," she added. "I didn't check anywhere else."

At that moment Nikki, Amber, and Haley walked into the lobby on a break from Silver Blades practice.

"Hey, Tee!" Nikki said cheerfully. "How's show biz?"

Martina was on the verge of tears. But she got hold of herself and told her friends what had happened. She wanted to tell them she suspected Tori, but how could she? These girls were Tori's friends, too. Even before they'd become Martina's friends.

"Did you check in your locker?" Amber asked. "Sometimes I put stuff in my locker without thinking. Maybe that's what happened to you."

"Let's go look," Blake suggested. He glanced at his watch. Martina didn't ask him the time, but she knew it must be after five. "Why don't you girls check the ballet room and the snack bar?"

The girls all nodded, then rushed off toward the ballet room. Martina and Blake headed back to the locker room. Along the way, Blake kept questioning her.

"Are you sure you had it before you went to get your skates?" he asked.

"Yes! I'm positive!"

"And are you sure you didn't take it with you when you went to get them?"

"Positive!" Martina repeated hysterically. "I put it on the bench, then left for about ten minutes. When I got back, it was gone!"

Martina made sure that nobody was getting changed in the locker room. Then she and Blake searched everywhere. As the minutes ticked by, all Martina could think about was Jake Collins. He'd throw another fit for sure! He'd yell and scream about how Martina had caused them to fall way behind schedule again. And she had a feeling that this time Jake wouldn't let it go.

Martina checked through her locker twice, then went back to the costume area. Kirsten had just come in. Martina asked her if she'd seen the costume.

"Not since I left it hanging on the hook for you," Kirsten replied.

Martina sank onto the locker room bench and put her head in her hands. Tears of frustration filled her eyes. She looked up as Nikki, Haley, and Amber came in. This time Tori was with them.

"Sorry, Tee," Nikki said, sitting next to Martina on

the bench. "We looked everywhere. Even the boys' locker room."

Martina looked at Tori, and the anger boiled up inside her. No more holding back, she told herself. She jumped up from the bench and glared at Tori.

"Did you check Tori's locker?" Martina asked angrily.

Tori wrinkled her nose. "What?" she asked.

"Don't pretend you don't know what I'm talking about!" Martina shouted. "*Your* locker! Your other plans to get me kicked off the movie didn't work, so you took my costume, didn't you?"

Tori seemed genuinely shocked by the accusations, but that didn't stop Martina. "Give it back, Tori!" she ordered. "I can get the janitor to open your locker, you know!"

"I don't know what you're talking about!" Tori snapped. "I didn't take your stupid costume!"

"Yeah, sure!" Martina snapped back. "Just like you didn't cut my laces or change the time on the info board, either!"

"What are you talking about?" Tori demanded again.

"Like you don't know!"

"I *don't*!" Tori insisted.

"Then how come you always seem to be hanging around when these things happen to me?" Martina demanded.

Tori's face turned even redder, and she seemed at a loss for words. Everyone stared at her, waiting for her to say something. Instead, she spun around and stormed off angrily.

Blake came up to Martina. "Come on, Martina," he

said quietly. "We have to tell Jake. We don't have a choice."

The knot in Martina's stomach was back and bigger than ever. It was time to face the director. She wasn't looking forward to this, not one bit.

Her friends walked her back to the entrance to the rink. No one said a word. When Blake ushered her into the rink, she turned to Nikki.

Nikki shot her a sympathetic look. "Good luck!" she mouthed.

Martina could hear Jake's angry voice before she could see him. When she did see him, he was yelling at a crew member.

Blake approached the director, and Martina watched him explain the situation. She moved closer to the two men, hoping to catch some of what was being said.

"It is *not* acceptable!" she heard Jake say.

She stepped forward and took a deep breath. "Uh, Jake? What if I skated in my workout clothes just for the rehearsal?" she suggested timidly.

Jake shook his head. "That won't work. The purpose of the dress rehearsal is to check the lighting and see how it reflects off you in costume."

Suddenly a voice came from behind them. "Martina?"

They all turned to see Vanessa Guzman.

"I just heard what happened," Vanessa said sympathetically. "Martina, you must be going out of your mind!"

Martina was stunned. Was Vanessa actually being *nice* to her again?

"Anyway," Vanessa went on, "why don't you wear my costume? It should fit, and it's the exact same costume. Then, after the rehearsal, we'll stage an all-out search for yours."

For the first time Martina felt hopeful. What a great idea! She spun around to see Jake's reaction.

"Go, go!" he ordered her, pointing to the locker room.

"Oh, thank you!" Martina cried. She breathed a sigh of relief, then raced back to the locker room with Vanessa close behind her.

"Thank you so much!" Martina cried as she tore off her clothes and put on Vanessa's costume. "I thought that was the end of me for sure! You saved my life!"

Vanessa smiled. "I just thought that if it was me, I'd die! So, what can I say? Anything to help."

Martina's hands shook as she zipped up Vanessa's costume. It didn't fit perfectly, but it was close. Then she checked her face in the mirror and cringed. Her makeup was totally wrecked! There were black smudges under her eyes from crying, and the powder base on her face had cracks in it. Oh, well, she thought, there's nothing I can do about it now.

By the time she had warmed up and was on the ice waiting for the music to start, Martina was a quivering mess. She couldn't believe how calm she'd been earlier that afternoon. Before she'd had a run-in with Vanessa at the snack bar. Before her shouting match with Tori. And before she'd discovered her costume missing. Now she was a bundle of nerves!

When the music started, Martina tried hard to forget what had happened and get into the routine. She took a deep breath and pushed off into a double salchow.

Only it was no use. She was still shaking and couldn't land the double salchow. What should have been a soaring jump became an awkward fall. Martina landed hard on her side. She sat there for a moment and tried to catch her breath.

"Cut!" Jake yelled. "Get up quickly, Martina! We don't have time to sit around!"

"Take two!" a production assistant shouted, snapping a clapboard a few feet away. The music started again, and Martina pushed into the double salchow for the second time.

And for the second time she fell.

"I'm sorry," she cried out nervously. "I'm just . . . I'm having trouble—"

"Cut!" Jake called again. His voice was impatient. Martina thought for sure she'd start crying again. She fought to hold back the tears. She picked herself up and got into her starting position for the third time.

"Take three!" the production assistant called out.

The music started, and Martina willed herself to calm down. Her heart was thumping wildly, and her legs were still shaking. She managed to complete the double salchow, but when she got to the Ramirez spiral, she was badly off balance. She landed on the ice with a loud thud.

No one said a word as Martina slid across the ice on her behind. When she slowed to a stop, she picked her-

self up and wiped the ice shavings from her costume.
A single tear slipped down her cheek as she took the
starting position for the fourth time.

"That won't be necessary," Jake said in a voice that
was tight with anger. "I'm instructing Blake to find another skater to take your place, Martina. You're fired!"

17

Jake's words cut through Martina like a knife. She got a sick feeling in the pit of her stomach, and she felt her face turn bright red. She knew she was going to start crying right then and there, in front of everyone.

Instead, she fled from the rink and into the locker room. Frantically she pulled off the costume and her skates and put on her street clothes. She ran from the Arena and headed up the street. She found a pay phone at a gas station and called her father to come pick her up. Then she slumped in a chair at the gas station and began to sob. She'd never been so unhappy—not to mention humiliated—in all her life.

Twenty minutes later her father picked her up at the gas station. Martina's eyes were puffy and red. Her face was streaked with tears. She got into the van and stared out the window the entire ride home. She couldn't bring herself to tell him the entire story, so she just said that she'd messed up and had been fired from the movie. At home, she ran upstairs to hide in her room.

She sulked in her room for over an hour until she heard a knock at her door.

"Come on, Tina! Open up!" It was Richard.

"Please!" Gabriella called out sadly.

Martina groaned. Her family was making her crazy. Couldn't they understand she needed to be left alone?

She heard Richard and Gabriella heading downstairs. A moment later there was a knock at her door again.

"Martina, I want to talk to you," Mr. Nemo said gently through the door. His voice was filled with concern.

Martina sighed. How could she tell him what had happened? He was probably so disappointed already.

"You can't stay in there forever, sweetie," he said.

Martina sat up and wiped her eyes. She stood and walked slowly to the door, opening it just a crack.

"You can come in," she said in a hoarse voice. "But I don't want to talk about what happened."

Mr. Nemo sat down on the edge of his daughter's bed. "You don't have to talk about it," he said gently. "But you might feel better if you did. You shouldn't keep things bottled up inside."

Martina sat next to her father on the bed. Her mother appeared a second later and sat on a chair across the room.

"How are you feeling, honey?" she asked.

"Peachy," Martina answered sarcastically.

Her parents exchanged worried glances.

"There's nothing anybody can do, anyway, so what's the point of talking?" Martina said.

"Maybe there *is* something we can do," Mr. Nemo said. "I spoke to Nikki a little while ago. She told me somebody stole your costume. Is that why they fired you?"

"Sort of," Martina said. She felt the tears welling up all over again. "But it wasn't my fault!" she sniffled.

The waterworks started again, and Martina let it all out. She cried for nearly five minutes straight. Then she tried to explain.

"And I kept messing up," she sobbed. "I just couldn't skate right, I was so upset. So the director fired me. In front of *everyone*! It was awful!"

Mrs. Nemo crossed the room and hugged Martina tightly. "That *is* awful," she said. "They have no right to treat you that way. I'm going down there tomorrow. I'll talk to that insensitive director . . . you can count on it!"

Martina started to protest. But then she realized she had nothing to lose. She'd already been fired from the movie. Why not let her mom talk to Jake?

The phone in Martina's room rang. Mrs. Nemo answered it. She placed her hand over the mouthpiece. "Your friends have been calling all evening. Why don't you talk to them? It might make you feel better."

Feel better? Martina thought. No way. Nothing could make me feel better right now.

Mrs. Nemo handed her the phone.

Mr. Nemo stood and ruffled Martina's hair. "We're here if you need to talk, okay?" he said. He kissed her forehead and left the room with her mother.

Martina wiped her nose and picked up the receiver. "Nikki?" she asked, still sniffling.

"Uh, no," a voice answered. "It's Tori."

Martina's stomach tightened. She sat upright in bed. "Tori?"

"Please just listen to me, Martina," Tori said quickly. "I know you probably want to kill me right now, but don't hang up. I have something important to tell you."

Martina said nothing.

"I didn't do any of those awful things!" Tori blurted out. "I swear!"

Martina still didn't speak.

Tori went on, talking a mile a minute. "You have to believe me. I would never do those things to you, Martina. Okay, I was jealous when you got cast in the movie—all right, *very* jealous—but I would never try to get you fired!"

"But you were always there," Martina began.

"It was because of my mother," Tori groaned. "You can't imagine what she's been like for the past few days! She's been on a mission to get involved in the movie in some way. It's so embarrassing! She knows the costume designer because they went to school together or something. She's been dragging me down to the set every day to show off a new costume. She wants Kirsten to recommend her to the director to design the costumes for his next movie."

So that explains the fashion shows, Martina realized.

Nikki was right—Tori's mother *was* up to something.

"Martina, I know I've been difficult lately," Tori went on. "And maybe a little obnoxious, too—"

"A little?" Martina asked with a laugh.

Tori laughed, too. "Okay, a lot! But I didn't do any of those things to you. Honest! I could never do anything like that to a friend."

Martina thought everything over. Tori had called her a friend. And she sounded sincere. Martina wanted to believe her.

"But that's not all," Tori said. "There's more." She took a deep breath. "I think I know what happened to your costume."

"You do?"

"But I can't tell you right now. Not until I'm absolutely, positively sure."

"Tori!" Martina cried. "You have to!"

"I can't," Tori said. "But I will. Tomorrow morning. Meet me at the rink before Silver Blades practice—and I'll explain everything."

Tori hung up. Martina stared at the receiver for a full minute before setting it down.

Why would Tori call her if she was really guilty of cutting the laces and changing the note? Tori must be telling the truth, Martina decided.

But one question remained unanswered.

If Tori hadn't done all those terrible things to Martina, then who had?

18

Martina adjusted her baseball cap so the visor came down to a point just above her eyes. She tucked her hair into the hat completely. It was the best she could do to disguise herself. She didn't want anyone to recognize her that morning. She wasn't ready to face anybody just yet.

She crept through the lobby of the Ice Arena and tiptoed all the way to the locker room. She held her breath as she opened the door, praying that Kirsten and the other movie people weren't there yet. Silently she slipped past two rows of lockers and stopped in front of Tori's.

Tori appeared suddenly from behind her. "I'm here," she whispered.

Martina's eyes widened as she saw that Nikki, Amber, and Haley were there as well. "What are you guys doing here?" she asked.

"Tori called us last night," Haley explained. "She has a great plan to get your role back! And we all wanted to help."

"She didn't tell us her plan until a few minutes ago," Nikki added. "But we had to help you, Tee."

Martina suddenly felt overcome with emotion. Her father had been right again—friends were the best for cheering you up. It felt great to know they were there for her. She gave them each a hug to show her appreciation.

"Okay, Detective Carsen," she said finally, putting her arm around Tori. "My mother is in the rink, giving Jake Collins a sample of the famous Nemo temper! What's *your* plan of attack?"

Tori laughed and gestured for the girls to follow her. She led them back out to the lobby and down the hall toward the coaches' offices. There was a narrow vestibule about halfway down the long hall. In the vestibule were a bunch of vending machines, a table, and a couple of chairs. On the wall was a window with a view of the parking lot out front.

Tori motioned for them all to be quiet. She took her place next to the window and peered outside. A few minutes later Tori waved them over to the window.

Martina and the others looked outside and saw Vanessa Guzman come out of her trailer. Vanessa was dressed in her copy of the yellow satin costume. She was walking toward the arena with a piece of paper in her hand.

Martina's heart fell when she saw the costume. "I

should be wearing that same costume right now," she whispered sadly.

Nikki put her arm around her friend. "Try not to think about it," she said gently.

They watched Vanessa enter the building. Then Tori frantically motioned for them to duck down behind a candy machine. They did, and seconds later Vanessa passed by in the hallway with a confused look on her face. When she was gone, Tori began to giggle.

"She's looking for the spare-blade closet." Tori snorted.

Martina stared at her. "There's no such thing," she said.

"Exactly!" Tori replied. "Now come on!"

Tori slipped back into the hallway, and the girls followed her down the hall and back into the lobby.

"I left Vanessa a note in her trailer," Tori explained quietly. "It said for her to meet Jake and Kirsten at the spare-blade closet to be fitted for special skates."

Martina's eyes widened. "You're kidding! You fooled her?"

"Yep!" Tori said with a grin.

"But why?" Martina asked. She was having trouble following all of this.

"To give us time to search Vanessa's trailer," Tori replied.

"Tori thinks Vanessa stole your costume, Tee," Nikki blurted out. "And we all think so, too."

Martina gulped nervously. Actually, the thought had crossed her mind as well. But she couldn't bring herself to believe it. Especially not after Vanessa had come to her rescue the day before.

"I'll explain it better in a minute," Tori said. "First we have to get into the trailer. Let's go!"

Tori led the way out into the parking lot and over to Vanessa's trailer. The girls double-checked to make sure no one was around, then, one by one, they crept through the open door.

The inside of Vanessa's trailer was pretty bare. Martina saw a bed, a kitchen area, a bathroom, and a closet. In addition, Vanessa had a huge makeup table covered with tons of cosmetics.

Tori kept her voice low as she spoke. "Remember how I told you my mother was making me hang around Jake to show off her costumes?"

Martina nodded. "Uh-huh."

"Well, the day you skated Luci's *Pirates* number so beautifully, I heard Vanessa tell Jake that she thought you were too short to play Luci."

"Really?" Martina asked. "Too short? Am I?"

"No, of course not," Tori answered. "I didn't really think anything about it, though, until the next time I sat there—the day Vanessa had a little trouble with her scene."

"A *little*?" Martina scoffed.

Tori laughed. "Okay, so I was being nice. Anyway, I was sitting pretty close to Jake that day, too. I could hear everything Vanessa was complaining about. And let me tell you, that girl had about a zillion complaints! She blamed her mistakes on everybody else—the lighting director, Kirsten, the makeup guy, the sound man! She even complained that the ice was too *cold*!"

Haley batted her eyes and mimicked Vanessa's voice. " 'Really, Jake, it'd be a lot more comfortable on this set if only the ice were warmer.' "

Tori grinned. "Can you imagine? Anyway," she continued, "Vanessa kept saying all these things to Jake. Like, shouldn't he have cast an older skater for the Luci role, and weren't you too young, or too short, or too thin, or whatever. She never had anything nice to say."

Martina shook her head in amazement. "And I thought she was so sweet!"

"Then after you acted that scene so perfectly," Tori said, "Vanessa just lost it. I heard her tell Jake she would quit if he didn't fire you!"

"Get out of here!" Martina couldn't believe it.

"That's when Jake told her to stop being such a baby. He also told her that if she didn't shape up, he'd fire *her*!"

"Wow!" Martina exclaimed.

"When I heard your costume was stolen, I suspected Vanessa. But I had no way to prove it. Since it ended up getting you fired, though, I decided it was time to *find* the proof." She gazed around the trailer. "And here we are."

"So why are we still standing around?" Haley asked. "Let's look for the evidence!"

Martina nodded, and the girls split up to search different corners of the trailer. The hunt didn't take very long. After thirty seconds of searching, Tori found the yellow satin costume under Vanessa's bed.

"Are you sure that's not Vanessa's costume?" Amber asked.

"She's wearing her copy of the costume," Tori reminded her.

"Let's go show it to—"

Martina didn't get to finish her sentence.

The door to the trailer flew open, and Vanessa appeared in the doorway. She was as surprised to see the girls as they were to see her.

"Wh-what are you doing in here?" Vanessa asked nervously.

Tori held up the costume. "We were looking for this!" she said boldly.

Vanessa shot a frightened glance at Martina. She broke down in tears. "Martina, please don't be mad," she begged.

Martina stared at her as if she were nuts. "After everything you did to me?"

"I am so sorry." Vanessa sat down on the couch and put her head in her hands. "I've been the biggest jerk ever since this movie started. I can't believe how I've acted."

Martina felt uncomfortable watching Vanessa cry. This was no act. Vanessa was really feeling lousy.

"Being sorry doesn't help Martina," Nikki pointed out. "You got her fired from the movie. But worse than that, you almost got her seriously hurt. Don't you know what could happen when you cut a skater's laces?"

Vanessa's head shot up and her red eyes widened. "I didn't mean to hurt you, honest! I was just hoping you would mess up."

Martina sat next to Vanessa. "How come you wanted me to mess up?" she asked.

Vanessa stared at the floor and wiped her eyes with a tissue. When she finally looked up, her face was flushed with embarrassment. "Because you were so *good*," she said quietly. "So much better than me. I was . . . afraid you were going to steal my part from me."

"Are you serious?" Martina asked. The thought of it almost made her laugh.

Vanessa sighed, then fell back onto the sofa. "It's happened to me before. You know that TV movie that came out last fall—*Man of My Dreams*? Well, I was supposed to be in it. But I got cut after a week of filming. The director said she wanted someone a little older."

"That's awful," Martina said sympathetically. "How could they just fire you like that, with no warning?" She slapped her forehead and grinned. "Never mind. I know the answer to that one!"

Vanessa frowned. "I know it's all my fault you got fired, Martina, and I feel terrible about it. Especially when I think about how I felt when it happened to me. That's why I confessed everything to Kirsten last night. She was going to go with me to explain it all to Jake." Vanessa swallowed hard. "I was just coming back here to get the costume."

"But I still don't get it," Martina said. "Why were you so afraid I'd steal your part? I'm not even an actress— I'm a skater!"

"Hey, from what I saw, you're not such a bad actress," Vanessa told her. "Watching you nail that scene the other day really scared me."

"I didn't mean for that to happen, Vanessa," Martina started to explain.

Vanessa stopped her. "No, don't be sorry! Jake asked you to do it. I know how hard it is to say no to Jake. He's a great director—even if he does get a little moody. Anyway, he was doing it to try to help *me*. He thought you'd understand Luci's emotion at that point in her life better than I would, since you're a skater and all. And he was right. You did."

"But you're a great actress, Vanessa," Martina said. The girls all nodded.

"We all love you on *Hollywood High*. When you had trouble with that scene the other day, you were just . . . having a bad day," Martina added, thinking about how much she sounded like her father.

"And anyway, I don't want to be an actress," Martina went on. "I want to be a professional skater. I've always dreamed of being in a grand ice show with flashy costumes and all that. Following Luci's life these past few days has made me realize it even more. I might have a career in the theater." She looked at Vanessa. "The *ice* theater, that is."

"Boy, am I relieved to hear that!" Vanessa sighed. She smiled and wiped her tear-streaked face. "Can you ever forgive me, Martina?" she asked hesitantly.

Martina was about to say "Sure" when Tori stepped up in front of Vanessa.

"She'll forgive you on one condition," Tori said sternly. "That you talk to Jake Collins and tell him what *really* happened!"

Martina arched her back and performed a perfect—well, *almost* perfect—Ramirez spiral. Her head was only inches above the floor. She was working hard to keep the position. But the gasp she heard from the crowd made the effort worthwhile.

The music ended, and Martina held the final pose an extra moment. She felt more like Luci Ramirez than she had at any other time during the whole ten days of filming. She had truly become one with her character.

Dad will be happy to hear that! Martina thought with a smile.

She straightened up gracefully. The applause that followed was the loudest she'd ever heard—even louder than it had been the time she'd skated Luci's *Pirates* number flawlessly. Then it had been a closed set. The only cheering had been from the cast and crew. But Jake had agreed to let her family and friends watch the filming of this special scene.

The cheering took a long time to die down. Martina grinned broadly as she gazed at the audience.

She waved to her friends in the bleachers. Nikki was practically doing jumping jacks. She was leaping up and clapping hard. Amber and Haley were stomping their feet. Tori and Vanessa whistled and jumped up and down like a couple of crazy fans. Even Andie Levine was cheering for Martina.

Martina turned to the very front row of the bleachers. Her entire family was going wild. Her father and mother were clapping and yelling, "Bravo! Bravo!" Richard, Gaby, and even Javier were jumping up and down with excitement.

Blake ran up to Martina and grabbed her in a giant hug. "That spiral!" he exclaimed. "It was nearly perfect!"

Martina grinned broadly.

Then her eyes caught Jake's. The director was smiling the biggest smile Martina had ever seen on him. He gave her a thumbs-up sign. Then Martina heard him shout five completely wonderful words:

"Fabulous, Martina! That's a wrap!"

school, has a plan that's sure to get her into *big* trouble. Could this be the end of Jill's skating career?

#5: The Perfect Pair

Nikki Simon and Alex Beekman are the perfect pair on the ice. But off the ice there's a big problem. Suddenly Alex is sending Nikki gifts and asking her out on dates. Nikki wants to be Alex's partner in pairs but not his girlfriend. Will she lose Alex when she tells him? Can Nikki's friends in Silver Blades find a way to save her friendship with Alex *and* her skating career?

#6: Skating Camp

Summer's here and Jill can't wait to join her best friends from Silver Blades at skating camp. It's going to be just like old times. But things have changed since Jill left Silver Blades to train at a famous ice academy. Tori and Danielle are spending all their time with another skater, Haley Arthur, and Nikki has a big secret that she won't share with anyone. Has Jill lost her best friends forever?

#7: The Ice Princess

Tori's favorite skating superstar, Elyse Taylor, is in town, and she's staying with Tori! When Elyse promises to teach Tori her famous spin, Tori's sure they'll become the best of friends. But Elyse isn't the sweet champion everyone thinks she is. And she's going to make problems for Tori!

#8: Rumors at the Rink

Haley can't believe it—Kathy Bart, her favorite coach in the whole world, is quitting Silver Blades! Haley's sure it's all her fault. Why didn't she listen when everyone told her to stop playing practical jokes on Kathy? With Kathy gone, Haley knows she'll never win the next big competition. She has to make Kathy change her mind—no matter what. But will Haley's secret plan work?

#9: Spring Break

Jill is home from the Ice Academy, and everyone is treating her like a star. And she loves it! It's like a dream come true—especially when she meets cute, fifteen-year-old Ryan McKensey. He's so fun and cool—and he happens to be her number-one fan! The only problem is that he doesn't understand what it takes to be a professional athlete. Jill doesn't want to ruin her chances with such a great guy. But will dating Ryan destroy her future as an Olympic skater?

#10: Center Ice

It's gold medal time for Tori—she just knows it! The next big competition is coming up, and Tori has a winning routine. Now all she needs is that fabulous skating dress her mother promised her! But Mrs. Carsen doesn't seem to be interested in Tori's skating anymore—not since she started dating a new man in town. When Mrs. Carsen tells Tori she's not going to the competition, Tori decides enough is enough! She has a plan that will change everything—forever!

#11: A Surprise Twist

Danielle's on top of the world! All her hard work at the rink has paid off. She's good. Very good. And Dani's new English teacher, Ms. Howard, says she has a real flair for writing— she might even be the best writer in her class. Trouble is, there's a big skating competition coming up—*and* a writing contest. Dani's stumped. Her friends and family are counting on her to skate her best. But Ms. Howard is counting on her to write a winning story. How can Dani choose between skating and her new passion?

#12: The Winning Spirit

A group of Special Olympics skaters is on the way to Seneca Hills! The skaters are going to pair up with the Silver Blades members in a mini-competition. Everyone in Silver Blades thinks Nikki Simon is really lucky—her Special Olympics partner is Carrie, a girl with Down syndrome who's one of the best visiting skaters. But Nikki can't seem to warm up to the idea of skating with Carrie. In fact, she seems to be hiding something . . . but what?

#13: The Big Audition

Holiday excitement is in the air! Jill Wong, one of Silver Blades' best skaters, is certain she will win the leading role of Clara in the *Nutcracker on Ice* spectacular. Until young skater Amber Armstrong comes along. At first Jill can't believe that Amber is serious competition. But she had better believe it—and fast! Because she's about to find herself completely out of the spotlight.

#14: Nutcracker on Ice

Nothing is going Jill Wong's way. She hates her role in the *Nutcracker on Ice* spectacular. And she's hardly on the ice long enough to be noticed! To top it all off, the Ice Academy coaches seem awfully impressed with Jill's main rival, Amber Armstrong. Jill has worked so hard to return to the Academy, and now she might lose her chance. Does Jill have what it takes to save her lifelong dream?

Super Edition #1: Rinkside Romance

Tori, Haley, Nikki, and Amber are at the Junior Nationals, where a figure skater's dreams can really come true! But Amber's trying too hard, and her skating is awful. Tori's in trouble with an important judge. Nikki and Alex are fighting so much they might not make it into the competition. And someone is sending them all mysterious love notes! Are their skating dreams about to turn into nightmares?

#15: A New Move

Haley's got a big problem. Lately her parents have been fighting more than ever. And now her dad is moving out— and going to live in Canada! Haley just doesn't see how she can live without him. Especially since the only thing her mom and sister ever talk about is her sister's riding. They don't care about Haley's skating at all! There's one clever move that could solve all Haley's problems. Does she have the nerve to go through with it?

Do you have a younger brother or sister? Maybe he or she would like to meet Jill Wong's little sister Randi and her friends in the exciting new series SILVER BLADES™ FIGURE EIGHTS. Look for these titles at your bookstore or library:

ICE DREAMS
STAR FOR A DAY

and coming soon:

THE BEST ICE SHOW EVER!
BOSSY ANNA